The Watchman of

Kerioth

a novel by
David Staines

Blessings.

[signature]

March 2016

Onwards and Upwards Publishers,
Berkeley House,
11 Nightingale Crescent,
West Horsley,
Surrey,
KT24 6PD

www.onwardsandupwards.org

Cover artwork: Sara Brembor
Editors: Hannah Settle, Zoë Muskett

ISBN: 978-1-910197-92-9

Printed in the UK by 4edge Limited

About the Author

David Staines was born in Buckinghamshire.

He provided the libretto for the musical 'Jack' (music by Robin Martin-Oliver) which received its professional première in 2007, and has written lyrics for many songs for the stage, schools and churches.

David has been a teacher, press officer, actor and singer, and throughout he has surrounded himself with books: from Elmer the Elephant to Aslan the Lion; from St. Exupéry to Shakespeare. He is currently Artistic Director of Parabola, a Christian theatre company, and works in communications in the charity sector.

David lives in Oxfordshire with his wife, Melinda, their son, Eliot, and a miniature pantera called Fiyero.

'The Watchman of Kerioth' is his first novel.

www.davidstaines.co.uk

Acknowledgements

I want to use these lines to just give thanks to a few people, but it must begin, as all begins and ends, with thanks and praise to my Lord, Jesus Christ – the foundation for it all.

I have been touched by the works of many great writers, and this book gives nods to Shakespeare, Virgil and Euripides. I thank them and many others for stirring an enduring love of the written word.

My writing career started as a child, penning dreadful plays with my dear friend Alex Hopkins for the 'entertainment' of our long-suffering parents. Alex has gone on to become an extraordinary writer who continues to inspire with his love for words and story, alongside steadfast friendship.

In more recent times I've been blessed by the literary and spiritual support of Megan Rowland and Heather Ramsey, two wonderful sisters in the faith who have challenged, inspired, and most importantly, believed! I also want to thank Steve Grimwade for his early encouragement with the book and giving me faith that I wasn't wasting my time!

My thanks too to Hannah Settle, Zoë Muskett and Luke Jeffery at Onwards and Upwards for their caring and detailed work on the text, and to Sara Brembor for her wonderful artwork.

Thank you to my parents, Ann and Dave, and sister, Sarah, who have always encouraged my creativity and have been unfailing in their love and support.

I am grateful to the children I taught at Leafield School who fuelled my love of great fantasy books, and also my nephews and nieces – Ethan, Levente, Anna, and Isaac – who I hope will read this when they are old enough, and particularly my amazing little prince, my wonderful son, Eliot.

Most especially though, I thank my beautiful wife and muse, Melinda, who has shown endless faith and patience in the book and its author; it would never have reached this point without her constant love.

This book is for her.

Preface

It started with a dream: a man upon a bench overlooking the sea, yet he is not a man, but something else. There is a castle, a fireplace, two children stood by, and there is a box. It's about the box. What is in the box? A secret, a secret so powerful as to change everything, forever.

I didn't imagine that a dream would still be resonating in my head, driving me on seven years later. It was about a quest, though, and I was on a quest of my own. There was a story to be told, and only I could tell it.

As the years went by, life changed, I changed: a full return to faith, becoming a husband, becoming a father. But through each season, the dream was still there, and now I share it with you.

Contents

How you have fallen from heaven, O morning star, son
of the dawn! You have been cast down to the earth, you
who once laid low the nations! You said in your heart,
'I will ascend to heaven; I will raise my throne above
the stars of God; I will sit enthroned on the mount of
assembly, on the utmost heights of the sacred mountain.
I will ascend above the tops of the clouds; I will make
myself like the Most High.' But you are brought down
to the grave, to the depths of the pit.

Isaiah 14:12-15

Prologue

THERE IS A DOOR IN THE WORLD.

For many thousands of years, countless numbers passed through the door. Humans and other beings passed into the world of spirits, and spirits walked freely into the world of men.

The two existed in perfect harmony until one spirit, an angel, grew weary of the established order, and sought to overthrow his Lord.

A great war followed, and many fell. The dark angel was defeated and his followers were banished from the world of spirits. And so they were exiled and doomed to serve their penance as prisoners of a mortal world, with time their only friend as they trod their lonely path toward certain death.

The door had closed. However, there was one who knew how to re-open it.

PART ONE

The Walking Shadow

·OΠε

MY GRANDFATHER WAS A DAEMON. That is to say, he was once good, but fell.

I have no memory of my grandmother, other than the memories that I created myself from old photos.

She died years before I was born. How she came to die I am to this day not certain. The past was spoken of seldom in our house. The secret shame of our family was oppressive in its silence, and so the memories that I had been denied became my plaything.

Two-dimensional, sepia memories took on a life of their own in my imagination. Anything was possible there: I was the creator of my own imagined kingdom; omnipotent, all-powerful. Anything was possible there. The dead could be brought back to life, and everyone could live forever.

Forever living in that motionless, momentary frame: the capture of a moment in time on a fragment of matted paper was my only link to the history that my sister and I had never known.

My grandfather had little time for us through our childhood. It wasn't something that we particularly lamented as we had no more wish to see him than he did us.

Distant, bitter, sarcastic and cruel were our living memories of him; cruelness that had caused suffering to so many who didn't deserve to suffer. When our governess, who by default had become our guardian, read the letter summoning us to our grandfather's house, it was something of a shock.

But what happened thereafter is the story I have to tell, because for all generations, it is the story of life and death and our enduring struggle for the eternal.

Two

HE STOOD ON THE BANK, looking out over the silent lake. The shroud of early morning mist bore down on his weary shoulders.

He had not seen this place for many a year, and yet it was hauntingly familiar. The gnarled willows overhanging the bank were now as twisted and pained, creaking in the gentle wind, as the arthritic knuckles of his once graceful hands. The dark lake, once glowing and brimming with life; now as dead and as black as his mournful old soul.

Was this really the place he had played in a bygone age; the place that used to echo with the sound of innocent laughter?

There was no laughter now.

It was little more than an empty shrine to the memory of a life he once knew.

No laughter now.

The only sound was the gentle lapping of the pungent water on the shingle bank. The water touched against his feet, coming up to the top of his shoes. He didn't move. The dark lake almost welcomed him.

'Darkness will soon take me,' he thought.

He leant heavily on his wooden cane. In recent years, that cane had become almost an extension of himself, the sole means by which he could move independently and also his weapon that he kept constantly at his side through the nights to ward off the imps and goblins that shattered his sleep.

Primo Aquila had once been a lean, powerful, athletic youth; as vital and energetic as the bright morning star; light in body and spirit.

The spirit had left him now. He was but a walking shadow. He awaited death with absolute trepidation, for he knew what lay beyond a mortal life for a soul such as him.

Nothing.

THREE

FEAR IS A TERRIBLE THING.

We are all afraid in one way or another; afraid of spiders, afraid of snakes. I know a girl who, would you believe, is afraid of custard. While I relish its creamy yellow smoothness, that velvety gloop as it caresses your throat, she freezes at the very sight of it; the same with jelly. Sadly she only discovered this after she started working at the pudding factory. I couldn't even mention the words "sherry trifle" without her having a fainting fit.

However, my point is that all of us are afraid of something.

Fear can protect us. It is how we avoid danger. If you stand on the high cliffs, like the ones at my grandfather's house at Kerioth, your fear tells you not to go near the edge, for you could fall and do yourself some terrible mischief.

Alas, it is also fear that inhibits us. It tells us not to go near the edge because we could fall... but also perhaps, not to go near the edge because we could fly.

The fear of achieving our potential. So we use fear as a crutch; an excuse not to do all that we can. An excuse not to try for fear that we might fail in our quest to succeed. An excuse not to do what is right, but what is easy.

Fear is the means by which the strong, and more-so the evil, control the weak.

Make the weak afraid that they will fall without you. Make the weak needy and reliant on you, and you can crush them. Fill them with promises of helping to fulfil their ambitions, bring them close and slowly suck ambition from them until they have no ambition other than to serve their master.

My grandfather knew this fear. This is how the great and powerful angel Primo Aquila became the feeble old horned man of this story; his energy and promise distorted out of all recognition by one who saw his weakness and twisted my grandfather's will to his own.

But I am ahead of myself, for as my grandfather stood on the bank, waiting to make his final mortal journey, I knew nothing of this tale, and the horrors my sister and I were to face could not have seemed further away.

FOUR

SINCE INFANCY, LUCIA, MY SISTER, AND I had been orphaned. How we came to be so is a story for another time, but as baby twins we were taken in by a gentle old spinster.

We could have been entrusted into the care of our one surviving relative, our grandfather, but he had no time for 'peevish brats', as he called us.

Angela Agnes Tibbs was a kindly old lady. She was a former school mistress, indeed we were told that she had taught my mother, but she was long since retired to her ramshackle old cottage in a little village in rolling hills in Middleofnowhereshire, where Lucy and I lived our idyllic, peaceful childhoods.

In the summer months the fields of rapeseed glowed golden in the evening sunshine as Lucy and I ran barefoot laughing and singing, often from some ruddy-faced farmer who had caught us picking fresh raspberries from his fields. They were the best of times.

We thought little of how we came to be orphans. We found it best not to ask. Miss Tibbs would clam up like a shell at the very mention of our parents, and the name of our grandfather was never spoken in her company.

'A wicked man, Joshua,' is all she would tell me.

I am Joshua, by the way.

Forgive my bad form in not introducing myself sooner. One thing you will learn through this story is that I have always been inclined to rush right in without observing the social niceties. Thankfully, my sister always had a more considered and considerate approach, which kept me in check and made us a formidable team!

Like all brothers and sisters we quarrelled now and then, but whether I admitted it at the time or not, hindsight and the mellowing of my impetuous youth in the intervening years has made me come to see that more often than not, my wise sister was right about so many things.

One Friday evening, Lucy and I were running, laughing down the single track dirt lane that was the only route in and out of the village, back toward old Tibbs' tumble-down cottage. The rough, golden stones of the buildings in the village just seemed to be haphazardly piled one atop the other without care for balance or structure. It was heaven!

We skipped down the lane. The only soul around was the milkman preparing his wooden cart for tomorrow morning's early round.

We kicked up the leaves and rooted around the hedgerows for fallen champion conkers.

It was the autumn of our thirteenth year and neither of us had any thoughts beyond the progress of our roughly constructed tree house and the worm farm we planned to install there.

What care could we have beyond his rural idyll?

As we turned the corner at the foot of the hill and came into view of what we called home, the ivy running wild over that higgledy-piggledy stone bunker, we saw the living room was illuminated by a roaring fire's glow, and Old Tibbs, we could see through the sash window, was not in her accustomed rocking chair, but was pacing anxiously, her form casting shadows as she tracked across the firelight.

'What time is it?' I asked Lucy as we neared the gate.

'Not yet five,' she replied. 'We can't be in trouble. We're not late at all.'

'Perhaps she's misplaced one of her wretched thimbles and thinks we've hidden it again!'

Miss Tibbs collected little porcelain thimbles. She had thousands. She would travel sometimes near a hundred miles to acquire a rare one, and every morning, so her routine went, she would clear the breakfast things and go to the dresser and polish and replace each of the blessed things. It took her until lunchtime.

We pulled up the latch on the sturdy old oak door (sometimes we thought the immense frame was the only thing that held the house up) and headed into the warmth.

The autumn nights had started to acquire a certain nip those last few evenings, and being twelve we had given little thought to being prepared for the cooling twilight.

The fire's glow welcomed us in.

As Tibbs heard our entry, she came to the living room door.

'Children, I have been waiting for you. Where the devil have you been?' she demanded in her clipped, authoritative way.

'It is only five o'clock, ma'am,' Lucy protested politely.

'Is it? Is it? Well, I...'

The old thing seemed oddly distracted as though she really had no idea of the hour. She turned to us again.

'Children, I think you had better sit down. I have some news that has taken me somewhat by surprise.'

We came in and sat down all the time shooting questioning looks at each other to see if the other had any clue what may have brought on the melodrama.

The prim old dear took a neatly folded sheet of expensive, embossed, cream paper from an envelope and read aloud.

FIVE

PRIMO AQUILA TAPPED HIS CANE impatiently against the side of his damp patent leather brogues. He removed his pocket watch from his tweed waistcoat and surveyed it, glancing intently at the ticking hands, which echoed now through his every meditation. He replaced the watch with an arthritic hand and again impatiently tapped his walking cane, as was his habit. Could it really be? Was it really slowing down? Though he constantly and furiously wound the thing to prevent it from stopping, still the mechanism seemed to lose pace with every passing day.

He knew what this meant.

For him, time was no great healer. Time had destroyed all, and now as he made his final earthly voyage, time was all that remained, though even that was scant.

'All these years upon the earth and now I have no blasted time! Damn you!' he muttered through gritted, sharpened teeth.

Who or what he damned was known only to him. The Pidaja? Old age? Maybe time itself incurred the old devil's wrath in that moment, but he was right of course. Blasted time was running out for him. As certain and constant as the motion of the water lapping at his feet, time marched on; stopping not for him nor any mortal.

Out of the gloom there came a sound, an inconsistent splashing of oars. The sound of the wooden face of the paddle slapping the water hard and a steady glug as the inexpert rower pulled back. There was a wheezing, too, as the vessel's sole crew member struggled to manoeuvre the creaking wooden craft to shore.

The pitiable boat came into view of my grandfather and he consulted his pocket watch once more before snapping at his faithful retainer: 'You're late!'

'Forgive me, Master,' replied the man as he shakily rose to his feet, unwinding his willowy frame and disembarking into the shallow briny and pulling the unseaworthy, rotten craft onto the shingle bank.

The servant wheezed again as he dragged the boat in, and pulled the vessel and himself up where he towered above his master.

Even in kyphotic old age he stood fully at six and a half feet tall. Time had wizened and emaciated his once muscular frame, but even now, when you feared the merest puff of breeze might topple him, he still had the air of a proud military man.

While his twisted old spine might not have allowed him to stand ram-rod straight as he once did, his movements carried a dignity of a once great man.

If his master's plan went well, he thought, however misguided and dangerous he considered it, he might even know greatness again.

He looked his mentor in the eye as he lent him a spindly, twig-like arm to steady the master as he ascended the vessel, and allowed himself a smile as his heart lifted to see Lord Aquila after months of isolation. The master returned the gesture.

'You are indeed a welcome sight, old friend.'

'Welcome home, sir,' offered the servant.

'Yes, I am going home. I will be returned to where I belong.'

Six

'SO, THERE IT IS,' finished Old Tibbs.

It is a painful cliché to say that my sister and I sat in open mouthed incredulity, but the thing with clichés is that more often than not they are terribly accurate, and so that is exactly what we did.

A shocked silence hung agonisingly in the air, only the crackle of the fire providing a slight relief from the deathly hush as none of the three of us knew how to break it.

In the end it was Tibbs' sly old cat, Astrador, who finally did break the dinful silence, jumping off Tibbs' favoured chair, sending it rocking back and forth, and toppling the iron poker that was propped by the fireside onto the flagstones.

'I don't like it, of course, and I have serious misgivings, but there is little, legally speaking, that I am able to do,' Tibbs finally spewed forth. 'He is your legal guardian, and as such, while you children are very dear to me and my home is yours, I have little option but to defer to his will.'

Lucia finally plucked up the courage to speak:

'I just don't understand. Why now? Why after twelve years of nothing should he suddenly want to see us?'

'I won't go,' I said sharply. 'I just won't go. He can't make us. We are happy here. We have everything we need. I won't go.'

'And neither will I!' Lucy exclaimed in kindred solidarity.

'Joshua, Lucia,' Tibbs began. She was addressing us by our full names, so we knew this was serious; 'I am delighted you feel so settled here, and goodness knows I have always done my best to make you happy–'

'And we are happy,' Lucy interjected, but Tibbs carried on, unhearing.

'However, your grandfather is most insistent that you should join him at your ancestral home and stressed that your attendance is of the greatest urgency. There really is very little we can do by way of protest, or to divert him from this course. I really am most terribly sorry.'

'You're not sorry!' I fumed. 'You're not sorry at all! If you wanted us to stay, you could make it happen, you just don't care what happens to us!'

I stormed upstairs rattling the ill-fitting bedroom door almost from its hinges.

It was childish behaviour, and I can only now offer up the defence that I *was* a child and didn't fully appreciate the situation that the old girl was in, or the power my seemingly decrepit old grandfather wielded.

After an hour or so of fuming and crying at my own impotence to do anything, my head buried under a pillow to block out the real world, there was a gentle knock at the door.

'What?' I barked from under my downy sanctuary.

Lucy entered and sat on the bed beside my prone body.

'We'll have to go, you know?'

'You've changed your tune!' I said petulantly, emerging from the pillow's protection.

'It's not Old Tibbs' fault, either.'

'I know that! I know that! It's just so unfair. Our lives are here, not in some dusty old castle with our dusty old grandfather. We have made our lives here. It's where we belong.'

'Is it though?' she replied.

I didn't answer. I didn't know how to answer such a question. Thankfully, Lucy put me out of my misery and continued.

'I mean to say, we have been cosseted and shut away from who we really are for all our lives. I love the life we have here, but aren't you just the tiniest bit curious about where we come from and how we came to be outcasts from our family? To find out what happened to our parents?'

'They died. That's all I need to know.'

'It's not an option, Joshie.'

'Don't call me that! You know I hate it when you call me Joshie! Josh or Jay. Is it so hard?'

'You really are a prat at times!'

'Oh, that's rich coming from Tibbs' little princess!'

'Oh stop it! Just stop it!'

There was silence and we both bowed our heads. After a second we both glanced up catching the other's eye, and we laughed.

While we fought like most brothers and sisters, being each other's only company had given us a sometimes grudging respect for each other, as well as a basic need not to fall out for long.

'We really don't have a choice, do we?' I mumbled in resignation.

'No. I don't think we do.'

'Alright. When must we leave?'

'First thing tomorrow. A carriage is coming for us.'

'Then I suggest we go downstairs, smile and enjoy beating Tibbs at chess, one last time!'

And that's what we did.

SEVEN

AS YOU CAN TELL FROM OUR REACTIONS, well, I grant you, mainly *my* reaction, the summons we had received had come as a shock to us all.

My grandfather had never attempted to make any contact with us throughout the twelve years of our lives, save for a couple of solicitor's letters Tibbs received in our infancy, placing us provisionally in her care.

Then after all those uncaring, negligent years he beckoned us to his side.

His letter had been uncompromising and showed none of the affection that you might expect of a prodigal guardian.

Tibbs,

Those peevish brats, the offspring of my son, are to be brought to me at Kerioth as a matter of grave urgency. My carriage will collect them at nine of the clock on Sunday and they are to wear their best. I will not receive them in the dirtied yokel rags that I am sure you have dragged them up in, you monstrous witch.
They need bring nothing else.
Do not expect to see them again.

Signed, this thirty-second day inst.
Primo, Lord Aquila, Watchman of Kerioth and Regent of the Nordland Range

From the snippets that Tibbs had shared with us of the old man, normally before biting her tongue and refusing to 'speak ill', it seemed that this was actually one of his more charming missives.

Tibbs tucked us in that night, something she hadn't done for some years, but we were glad of those brittle old hands stroking our brows and pulling the counterpanes reassuringly to our chins, covering us in a blanket of affection.

Despite the safety of that old cottage, I wasn't to sleep that night.

Although we had rooms of our own, Lucy wanted to sleep in mine that night, so Tibbs had made up the camp bed alongside my own.

We settled without a word, but I just lay there, staring at the peeling plaster on the jaundiced ceiling.

I want to write here that my mind was racing, swimming with emotions and thoughts of what was to come, but in truth I don't recall any thought or emotion at all. Just a numbness; a kind of empty grief for the happy life that I had known and a terrible resignation to the fact that my life would not be the same again.

My innocence was lost in that dark, sleepless night.

I think until that point, I really did believe that my utopian, idyllic life away from the dangers of the world (save for the occasional angry, ruddy-faced farmer!) would last forever.

My childhood was over.

I could tell that Lucy was sleeping only fitfully too, but we spoke not a word.

One of the wonders of being twins was our unspoken symbiosis of thought and feeling. There were times when we didn't need words. However, in that silence of unity, I knew that Lucy was as totally lost in numb senselessness as I.

EIGHT

THE WIRY SERVANT PUSHED OFF from the bank and climbed aboard, curling his lank frame into the rowing seat.

His passenger looked vacantly into the distance as the misty lake glowed dimly with the first light.

'Luciferi primo cum sidere frigida rura carpamus, dum mane novum, dum gramina canent.'

'Master?' questioned the uncomprehending servant. The master sighed and then translated:

'Let us hasten, when first the morning star appears, to the cool pastures while the day is new, while the grass grows dewy.'

He stopped momentarily, lost in reverie, and then was suddenly alert.

'Hasten, fool! Hasten! This day of days has begun.'

THE LAKE WAS STILL, and eerily silent as the two men slowly moved their way through the fog.

Even against the gentle current, the servant Picardo struggled to make progress and every stroke was tortured. His master was impatient to travel quickly, but despite his earlier rebuke, remained silent, showing an unusual degree of understanding that his man-servant no longer had the strength to glide the craft effortlessly across the water as once he did.

Despite the familiarity of the place, Primo Aquila felt uneasy as they continued their silent voyage. The lake where he swam as a youth was covered in a blanket of dense fog, and the only sound, but for oars splashing clumsily into the water, was a deer running distantly through a field, an otter sliding into the water, or maybe a beaver, maybe a snake, or maybe a monster. His mind ran away with him, before he regained himself and spoke aloud in affirmation: 'There are no monsters here.' But he knew, within himself, that this was now a place of shadows, and in those shadows dwelt things he could not bring himself to think of.

His impatience finally got the better of him, 'Hurry, damn you! I am anxious to be indoors by nightfall. This place is not safe after dark.'

'Yes, my Lord,' the honest servant proffered eagerly, though he already paddled with all his might. He knew from bitter experience that there was little to be gained from arguing with his cantankerous master, and even if there were, he had no desire to be at enmity with the old man, not now. Not now.

In any case, even if there were anything to gain, and he did feel inclined to protest, he had barely the breath for rowing, and at his stage of life, breath was at a premium!

He had served his master, Primo Aquila, for his whole adult life and had been the sole companion of the old man since 'the unpleasantness'.

Save for that blasted pocket watch that the master would never be parted from! Constantly checking it, winding it, as though he were afraid that if it were ever to stop, it would be the end of the world!

You would not believe it now, but in his prime, Antonius Picardo had been a great man. Despite his lowly birth, he was held in an esteem usually reserved for the upper echelons of society. An educated man, an aesthete, and a formidable athlete. Ironically, rowing was once his forte. Would that he could have now wound back the clock twenty years, as he struggled against the swell.

His athleticism served him well in adulthood, as a fine warrior and leader of men. The tragedy of his greatness was that he loathed war. He was a pacifist, forced to kill out of fear. His loyalty outweighed his conscience. He switched off emotion in battle and became a machine programmed only to triumph at whatever cost.

The price of his steeliness was to become a lack of feeling, but for the man he served. Despite being the desire of many a woman, he never married. Duty and honour were his wife, and the uneasy union of master and servant his only lasting relationship of note. Since her...

He looked now through the shroud of mist at my grandfather. The master did not catch his eye. Would not catch his eye. So much they had seen together, so much they had shared. And now in the twilight of their lives, they had nothing to say. No whimsical anecdotes. No good-hearted banter. Only regret. Only regret, and so they continued their journey in silence.

As they stealthily but slowly moved across the lake, a shadow appeared in the fog before them. At first it was indistinct, but then as they drew closer its towering majesty was unmistakable to Primo Aquila.

Kerioth.

He could not recall a time when he hadn't known this place. It had been the scene of so much happiness, but he had no memory of that now. Dark secrets lurked here. Secrets that must be cracked open but he had so little time, for just as he drew his first earthly breath within those walls, he knew he would surely breathe his last therein also.

Time. So little time. Four and a half thousand years he had been upon this earth, and the whole journey would boil down to this. Hours, minutes, seconds.

He took his watch again from his pocket, checking the time, and winding it just a few millimetres. Not once in all the years of his earthly life had the mechanism stopped. Not once. Primo Aquila would not allow it to now either.

NINE

THE FIRST LIGHT CREPT THROUGH the faded curtains and I knew that I had yet to fall into the blissful embrace of sleep.

As I looked across to the camp bed beside me, light dappled the covers and I could tell that Lucy had succumbed to tiredness, and without sound, so as not to disturb her, I rose and lithely climbed over the makeshift bed.

She slept like an angel, lying there, her golden hair tousled, lying in pre-Raphaelite curls over the pillow. She looked so beautiful.

I say this last without modesty. As twins we looked very much alike. My own handsome features were topped with a mop of flaxen waves, which Tibbs called my crowning glory!

I lifted the creaking latch on the old wooden door as soundlessly as I could (which wasn't all that soundlessly, the truth be told). Lucy stirred slightly and murmured momentarily before drifting back to the land of nod from whence she had come.

I made my bare-footed way out into the corridor. The stone floors of the old cottage pressed cold against my unfettered toes.

The corridor ran the length of the house, and even at the age of twelve my head was mere inches from the low oak beams that traversed the passageway like rail track sleepers.

Along the walls (wood on one side, stone on the other) were a series of portraits, landscapes and assorted still lives of varying quality.

Before her retirement, Tibbs had told us she was an art teacher (although I have since had cause to doubt the absolute veracity of this point). She took pride in her private gallery. Some of the works were her own, others the creation of friends and students.

While she had aged greatly in these past couple of years, the Tibbs of my infanthood had been lithe and graceful, almost seeming to float as she breezed down the hallways in flowing, bohemian dresses. Now cardigans and a blanket across the knees were her uniform of choice.

Some of the paintings that adorned the house were of her. Although brittle and frail now, she had been very beautiful.

At the end of the small kitchen garden that adjoined the cottage there was a tumbledown shed that Tibbs used as a workshop. She had made the place out-of-bounds to Lucy and me, which, of course, only served to pique our interest.

One morning when she had taken a hansom into the nearest town to purchase a rare, antique Yaponaise hand-painted thimble which had belonged to the mistress of Emperor Ishi-Bashi or something like that, Lucy and I ventured into the forbidden area.

It was a cobwebbed, mildewy shack. The damp smell was only overpowered by the noxious aroma of turpentine.

The workbench overran with discarded brushes and pallets, and there was a potter's wheel, clogged and encrusted with flaking, unused clay. There was a pair of pinewood easels at the centre of the room, loaded with half-finished canvasses.

The shed structure was a lean-to with one side being comprised of the stone garden wall, and it was there that we saw an extraordinary beauty.

In a crafted, gilded frame was a portrait of an unclothed young woman. She lay, body facing away from the viewer, but her head turned back. The silken skin of her beautiful back and slender neck leading to a porcelain face, the gentle drape of a satin sheet casually lying, obscuring her rear and the tops of her thighs, was almost opalescent in quality.

The painting seemed to have an energy which made you feel that you could reach out and touch the angel who was painted there. It was my first experience of the female form and it was remarkable.

Both Lucy and I moved instinctively closer to this magnum opus of portraiture and then recoiled slightly at the sudden shock of recognition. The beautiful young woman in the picture was unmistakable: *Angela Agnes Tibbs.*

Lucy and I never spoke to Tibbs of what we had found. We assumed that she was too embarrassed to keep the thing in the house, but we made regular visits down to the shed to behold its beauty.

However, what did happen is that more and more we noticed around the house that women in crinoline dresses, women under parasols, women at tables in cafés, in rowing boats, literally dozens of pictures by as many different artists, all bore the same features. Tibbs.

She had an iridescent beauty and seemed to inspire the artistic mind. This dear, sweet old lady had clearly lived a life that we had never imagined.

'That's you in that painting, isn't it, Miss Tibbs?' I'd once enquired, pointing to a dreary canvas of women carrying umbrellas in a deluge.

'Yes dear. It is.'

'And you're in that one too,' Lucy added, surveying a dotted landscape of bathers on a sunny Sunday afternoon.

'Yes, that is also me.'

'You were very pretty,' said Lucy

'Thank you, dear. I was very blessed to know very many talented people with whom I was able to work, and sometimes maybe, setting modesty aside if you'll allow me that indulgence, inspire just a little.'

'I think they are wonderful,' said my smiling sister.

'Yes, they are. And I have wonderful memories of wonderful times, but time moves on, and I have other wonders to occupy me now,' Tibbs said, putting an arm around each of us.

As I looked at the dotty painting on that last morning in the cottage, a tear came into my eye. Dear, dear Tibbs. After this, I expected never to see her again, and that my memories would be all that I have left of her.

Memories of the painted lady!

'DON'T REMEMBER ME IN OILS AND CANVAS.'

The voice came from behind me and I turned to see Tibbs standing watching me in a dressing gown and slippers.

She held Astrador, purring contentedly in her arms. His elderly feline breath was almost an asthmatic wheeze.

'Don't frame memories in a cold, still image of a time past. Let your memories live!'

'I'm not sure I understand, miss.'

'When I remember you, Joshua, after you have left here, and I will remember you, dear heart, every day. I won't remember a photograph or something that happened long ago. I will think of you as I imagine you are, not as my failing old brain thinks you once were. Simply because I cannot see you any more does not mean that you are any less real, or that you cease to exist.'

'I think I understand, but what about when people die? What about my parents? All the memory I have of them is in photos.'

'Dear Joshua. You are separated from your parents only by physical distance, just as you will be from me. Death is not the end. In your heart they are very much alive. In spirit they are close to you, and always will be, as I will be. Those we love never truly leave us, and so while I will remember you, I will not miss you, because I will feel your spirit close by.'

'Oh Tibbs, I wish I didn't have to leave this place. Leave you.'

'Joshua, I wish the same, but sometimes our heart's desire is not always what is best for us. Sometimes the hardships we face make us the people we are meant to be, as difficult to understand as that may seem. Whatever your grandfather's intentions, if you keep the thought of those you love close by, and if you are true to what you know to be right, no harm will come to you.'

With a gentle leap, Astrador fell out of Tibbs' arms, allowing me to fall into them. The moggy brushed affectionately at my legs before going to the open bedroom door from which Lucy now emerged.

Tibbs removed herself from my clinging embrace and I saw her wipe a tear from behind her wire-rim glasses. She straightened herself, regaining composure to say with the calm authority of the natural teacher she was: 'It is time to get ready, children.'

Ten

WE STOOD CEREMONIALLY in the living room. Lucy pretty in a gingham dress, long, white socks and her hair tied and pinned neatly back. With her shoulder bag she looked very grown up.

I, on the other hand, looked a fool! As I coyly looked down at my highly-polished shoes I saw my ghastly reflection.

My freckled face, gawping, was topped with a cloth school cap. I didn't go to school, of course, Tibbs taught us at home, but she had dug the relic out of some old chest and plonked it atop my wavy locks.

Further down, I donned a crisply laundered shirt and tie which was cloaked with a grey, woollen blazer that may have fitted me two years ago. The overly snug tailoring hunched my shoulders upwards and gave the impression of my having enormously long arms where the sleeves rode up just below the elbow. Even my slender frame threatened to pop open the one remaining button with every breath.

The baggy flannel cloth of my short trousers held aloft, and dignity saved only, by the grace of some garish braces, completed my mismatched ensemble.

Whatever my grandfather's faults, thought I, surely the old man would save my blushes from such a frightful wardrobe as this.

'Not bad. Not bad at all,' considered Tibbs as she walked back and forth like a geriatric schoolmistress-cum-sergeant major in her living room parade ground.

Lucy tried not to giggle as the ill-fitting blazer pinched my shoulders into a most unmilitary bearing and the stitching threatened to give way at my every movement.

'Yes, let it never be said that I ever let you be less than neat or tidy. You both look very handsome, very handsome indeed.'

Lucy sniggered, but I was too straitjacketed to carry out my wish to jab my bony elbow into her rib in childish retribution.

Besides, our attention was distracted by the sound of a carriage pulling up outside. There followed the tattoo of footsteps on the gravel pathway and then a sturdy knock on the front door.

Tibbs looked at us both with a mixture of trepidation and reassurance. We stared blankly back with only the former in our eyes.

Astrador was the first to the hallway, scratching and snarling at the entrance in animalistic instinct at what unpleasant fellow may lurk upon the other side.

Expertly, Tibbs side-footed the moggy gently with her slippered foot out of her path and lifted the latch and let the oak door swing open.

Lucy and I had read a lot of books for a pair of twelve-year-olds – Tibbs had insisted that we stimulate our imaginations on the long country nights – and the sight before us now, I am saddened to tell you, was the very epitome of children's adventure book 'baddies'. A walking, talking cliché of malevolent smarm. An oily, slippery, clammy-skinned, bug-eyed, pin-striped portrait of obsequiousness.

Lucy and I stood dumbstruck as the toad-like figure doffed his bowler, revealing a balding pate sparsely populated with slick black hairs. He gave a well-rehearsed, ingratiating little bow.

Lucy spoke first. 'Grandfather?'

The toad gave a little chuckle, or maybe more of a croak, and moved his white-gloved hand coquettishly to his mouth.

'I am afraid I do not have that very great honour,' slimed Mr. Toad, 'I have the pleasure of conducting your dear grandfather's business and legal affairs. I am Innocent Quibble, Lord Aquila's lawyer, and your grandfather has bestowed on me the very great delight of welcoming you to his care and escorting you on your journey to Kerioth.'

His richly honeyed words left me stone cold. A lawyer? It was hard to see how any courtroom judge or jury could not see through his pathetically insincere charade.

'Now, it is a long journey to Kerioth and your grandfather is eager that you should meet him with all expediency. So we should best "make tracks" as they say!' He gave a little croak of self-appreciation as if he had said something amusing.

'Who are "they"?' I questioned, looking him square in his bulging orbits.

'Forgive me, young man, I don't understand.'

'You said "as they say" and I just wondered who "they" were that said that?'

The portly amphibian creature looked stumped at my doe-eyed innocence and stuttered as I allowed a smirk to touch upon the corner of my mouth.

Tibbs rounded on me with a glare that both scolded and congratulated my mischief making.

'Brrr,' the fat fool flustered, showering droplets of spittle across the hallway. 'Umm, right, well, we must away. Have you been to the lavatory, children? I'm afraid we shall be quite unable to stop en route.'

'The children are prepared for their travels, Mr. Quibble. They are house-trained, you know?'

Lucy and I fought to suppress our giggles as Tibbs rebuked the greasy little man.

'Err, capital. Capital!' He mumbled, touching a silk handkerchief taken from his top pocket to his lips to dab at a fresh batch of saliva that now emanated from the corner of his wide mouth. 'Well, come along!'

As he turned, he unceremoniously tripped over Astrador, who had taken up residence behind him, falling flat on his bloated face on the shingle pathway.

Astrador then coolly raked his claws across the toad's ankle, causing him to howl in pain. Astrador simply turned and gave a little nonchalant wiggle of his rear end, as cats do, and if I didn't know better, I'd have sworn that he winked at me!

Still grinning at the slippery toad's slip, Lucy and I now turned to Tibbs.

'Now Joshua, as I have told you, the hardships we face make us who we should be. Do not look back. Look to the present and to the future, and there find your happiness. Those we love never truly leave us.'

We fell into her warm embrace and without a further word walked along the path and reluctantly stepped into the ink-black carriage. When we finally looked back to give Tibbs one last wave, the door was closed.

The way back was blocked. The only way now was forward.

ELEVEN

THE COACH DRIVER WHIPPED the two elegant black steeds into action, and we were on our way.

We were surprised when we entered the carriage to find it was already occupied.

'Children, allow me to introduce you to my son, Quibble Minor.'

The small form of Quibble Minor turned away from the window through which it had been gazing, and looked at us now with horrible black eyes.

Quibble Minor could have been no more than six years old, and yet he was a curious sight to behold.

He was dressed, like his father, in pinstripes, but his visage was shockingly different.

Above the black, soulless, shark-like eyes sat a single thick, dark eyebrow. His young cheeks, not rouged, rounded and cherubic like a normal six-year-old, but covered in wiry hair. The cheekbones were prominent and the eyes sunken into the skull. His ears were rounded and protruding, emerging through the thick, coarse black hair that covered his head.

He was more chimp than child, and as he malevolently smiled in greeting, he revealed a mouthful of teeth like a bag of rusty nails.

Perhaps I am doing the poor little chap a disservice, and he may now have grown into a handsome buck with a beautiful wife. But he truly was an ugly little runt!

'I know that you children have not had much company of peers in your country prison...'

'Prison!' I seethed under my breath, but let the toad continue:

'Quibble Minor too has lacked playmates. Mrs. Quibble and I found it better to keep him indoors. He doesn't care much for sunlight and he does have a fondness for biting things...' He trailed off as I imagined the monkey-boy gnawing the leg of some poor infant. 'However, now you shall be virtual neighbours, although my little house is much more humble than Lord Aquila's magnificent estate, I thought it might be nice for you all to be friends.'

Lucy and I looked appalled, while chimp-child looked delighted, flashing what passed for a smile from his corroded jagged teeth, and holding out a hairy hand in friendship.

Lucy, being a somewhat more compassionate soul than I, surveyed the creature and then offered her hand.

The younger Quibble gently took her hand in his, staring in silent wonder at her smooth, flawless skin. He tenderly cupped his other hand around, stroking the porcelain beauty of my sister's fingers. Then with a primitive howl he ducked his head down and sunk his mismatched teeth into her ivory flesh.

Lucy screamed and the carriage jerked as she kicked back against l'enfant terrible.

'Let go, Quibble Minor!' Quibble Major yelped, trying to drag the simian youth from my sister. 'Down!'

At the command, he let go and retreated to sit panting at his father's feet like an obedient dog.

Lucy collapsed back into the seat as the toad wrapped a restraining leg around the monkey. I took a defensive position sitting between my sister and her assailant.

'I'm most terribly sorry, Miss Lucy. He is trying to be friendly, but is slightly misguided as to what is a socially acceptable greeting. Can I get you a bandage for your hand? I really am most terribly sorry.'

'It's fine,' said Lucy. 'He didn't draw blood. Please think nothing of it.'

Think nothing of it? It's fine? It wasn't fine! I really never understood my sister's compassion.

I was ready to kick the little brute to within an inch of his life, but maybe our different characters made us all the more suitable for the roles we were to play in the time to come.

'You called him Quibble Minor,' I said now to the senior Quibble.

'Yes.'

'But you called him Quibble Minor? Does he not have a first name?'

'Ah, well, no. I am afraid he doesn't. When Quibble Minor was born, it appeared most unlikely that he would survive infancy, and so Mrs. Quibble and I never named the boy. He continued to be sickly as a youth and we... well... we never got round to it, one might say.'

'Everyone has a first name,' piped up Lucy. 'Everyone has to have a first name. It's who we are, part of our identity, what makes us individuals.'

'Perhaps you are right. Maybe we should name the boy.'

Minor smiled his terrible smile, as I swear in that moment he experienced for the first time what might have passed for love.

JUST IN THAT MOMENT between father and son, I saw a glimmer of humanity in Innocent Quibble. It was a fleeting feeling, alas.

The journey continued in near silence. The constant rhythm of the horses' hooves and the wheels of the carriage became the soundtrack to the next couple of hours.

Infrequently, Quibble Major would give one of his effeminate little coughs, each time feyly covering his mouth with his white-gloved hand.

Quibble Minor seemed to relax as the journey wended its way onwards, gazing intently at Lucy and me as we went along, bashfully turning to the window if we caught his stare.

I felt a twinge of sadness for the little ape. One couldn't help but feel that he had been deprived of any affection and even human company through his life.

It was entirely possible that Lucy and I were the first children he had seen, perhaps even the first humans beyond his parents.

Although I could only see her out of the corner of my eye as I slouched back into the firm red leather upholstery of the carriage, Lucy was clearly tense.

She had little give-away signs. Biting her top lip with her lower teeth, until the tiny stray freckle was sore, and also the gentle patting of one hand on the other as they sat on her lap, as a little gesture of self-reassurance.

I sat opposite the elder Quibble who was clearly deeply uncomfortable at the thought of making small-talk with children. I did wonder if Quibble the senior had ever been a child himself at all, or whether he was born fat and middle-aged.

He made one or two attempts to start conversation, but Lucy and I gave him little to feed off, giving short answers or grunts to his awkward questioning.

So, against the backdrop of this tedious, nervy silence, I spent much of the time staring out of the window as the countryside rattled past.

We lived with Tibbs in Middleofnowhereshire, and the name was apt, and yet the further we journeyed, the more remote from civilisation we seemed to become.

Immaculately tended fields of rape and barley with neat stone walls dividing the patchwork of colour, honey coloured cottages and sunny, bustling villages began to give way to something more rugged.

Lucy and I had never travelled this far before. That makes it sound as though we had been insular in our lives in our little cottage, but far from it. There we had everything we needed, and we had the arts and our imaginations, which spread wider than any kingdom or dominion that the greatest pioneers and explorers could ever discover!

However, the newly sparse landscape was unfamiliar to us. Steep escarpments and rocky crevasses passed on both sides. The road curved and became uneven as we scaled slopes, which became hillsides, which became mountainsides.

Wide rivers ran wild and white over bouldered valley bottoms. Shepherds' huts perched precariously like stony tombs that had been abandoned for centuries.

The palest blue autumnal sky gave way to metallic grey, interrupted by the silhouetted turrets of iron-cast mountains. Inhospitable steeples, cold, unwelcoming and devoid of life.

The coach started to head downhill and in the far distance I could see the coastline, though the icy sea was near indistinguishable from the grey sky it reflected.

'I know this place!' I let out, almost involuntarily, as a fiercely cold chill came over me. Although I could have no memory of this land, its familiarity was disturbingly real to me. Visions of times past. Visions of battles, pain, anger, death... my parents.

Yes, my parents!

'They were born here, weren't they?' I said, looking to Quibble.

He refused to meet my eye, looking instead out of the window before replying: 'Yes. Yes, that's right,' he hesitated, 'and they died here.'

'Stop the coach! Stop it now! I want to go back. I don't like this place.' Lucy had been silent for so long that the sound of her voice startled me as she let forth a torrent of fears and tears.

'I'm afraid that's quite impossible, my dear. Lord Aquila is expecting you imminently. I am quite sure that when you are in the castle and settled into your quarters, you will feel much more at ease.'

'Just let me out!' Lucy went for the carriage door, jamming the handle down. I made to stop her but it was too late as her momentum took her forward and she tumbled part way through the opening, the door swinging and hitting her in the face.

The Quibbles and I managed to grab her ankles as she lay screaming, her torso hanging like a ragdoll out of the carriage which still plummeted forward along the uneven mountain road. Her arms hung down, knuckles scraping the coarse dirt track and her body swinging pendulously with the movement of the vehicle, perilously close to its spiked metal wheels.

Keeping one hand on her ankle, Quibble Senior grabbed his cane with his free hand and rapped violently on the roof of the carriage to alert the hooded driver to the unfolding drama.

'Stop, man! Stop!' he yelled in vain as the carriage continued unabated in its progress, my sister bobbing out of the side like a helpless creature being bitten and shaken to its death in the jaws of a monstrous crocodile.

'Stop! Stop!' Quibble the elder pleaded. I joined his mercy cries and even the monkey child emitted some unintelligible shriek of anguish.

With a sudden jerk we were all launched forward as the coach came to a juddering halt. We clattered into the walls and Lucy was tossed head first from the doorway as we lost our fragile grip.

I regained myself and leapt from the wagon to find her spread-eagled in a bed of hedgerow. I pulled her into my arms and she opened her eyes and faintly smiled.

Her golden hair was matted and shabbily draped across her forehead, streaked with crimson. Her nose dripped red, her eyes swollen, and her delicate hands grubby and scraped.

'Oh, dear, gracious me! What will your grandfather say?' said Quibble emerging from the coach. 'We must get you cleaned up.'

With that he issued instructions to the driver and we were soon in a small wooden barn, which I assumed to be a far-flung part of my grandfather's estate.

A tap in the yard allowed Lucy a chance to clean away the blood and grime, and then we were on our way again.

All of a sudden, the terrible thoughts I had of this place and the images of my parents' deaths didn't seem quite so vivid. For I was instead filled with gratitude that, for then at least, this land, this field of bloodshed, was not to claim my sister's life as well.

Twelve

'IS ALL PREPARED?'

'Yes, my Lord. I have made up the rooms and the Átjáró Chamber is ready for your use.'

'I do so wish that I could go myself, Picardo. To leave my fate in the hands of peevish children is hardly fitting and leaves much to chance.'

'You will return, Master, when the time comes. You will return and claim what you desire. The children have their advantages...'

My grandfather considered the uses he could make of my sister and me. The nefarious schemes he had in mind were still unknown to us as our carriage swung off the main road and through the gateway to Kerioth.

LUCY SAT IN SHAKEN SILENCE beside me. Her hand, raw with grazes and welts, gripped mine tightly as we entered the estate.

The metallic sky had fractured slightly to reveal a chink of blood-red evening light. It was dusk and we had travelled all day.

The wonderful life we had left behind seemed a lifetime away from this desolate place.

Imposing iron gates, entwined with thorny creeping plants stood open as the coach careered through.

Along the driveway, at regular intervals, there stood marble statues on granite pedestals. Grotesque effigies of griffins, dragons or some other beasts.

They stood white against the perilous dark sky, but their pallor was tired, jaded, caked in years of decay and neglect.

As we drew closer I could see that these figures were not of beasts at all, but of men, hideously disfigured, vandalised. Some missing heads, arms, some with shattered protrusions from their backs where something had been violently hacked from once beautiful carvings.

Wings?

Of course, wings. They were angels. Holy artworks butchered, but for what cause?

What? The wings cut off to make them appear like men? Make them as mortals?

Why would anyone do such a thing?

Lucy seemed not to notice, still lost in thoughts of her fearful journey. Quibble sat in uneasy silence and his child had fallen into a fitful sleep beside him.

My apprehension was growing and I had no-one with whom to share it. What I'd have given for Tibbs to be there. Dear, wise Tibbs.

As the coach pulled up abruptly, Lucy became suddenly alert.

'Are we here?' she asked timidly, sounding not a bit like herself.

'Not quite,' Quibble came back, 'the coach has taken us as far as it can.'

We unsteadily alighted, the hours of travel making our legs weary from their inactivity.

We looked up to see a man, a giant of a man to our childish eyes, gangling, bent and aged, standing by a battered old rowing boat. Quibble spoke:

'Children, please allow me to introduce you to Antonius Picardo, your grandfather's manservant.'

'Master Joshua. Miss Lucia. Welcome to Kerioth.'

Thirteen

TO DESCRIBE KERIOTH AS A SOULLESS PLACE would be to miss the point.

Although it was desolate, sparse and decaying, it seemed to silently scream with the sound of a million souls, a million memories.

It was a place that simply reeked of sadness. That odourless stench of shattered dreams, crushed illusions, pain and death.

The still, dull water, lit only by our oarsman's lamp, seemed to hide a silent terror. That beneath the surface hid some monstrous basilisk of a terrible memory.

Tibbs had frequently told me that often the hearts of even the bravest of men, below their calm exterior, raced uncontrollably. So it was with the lake. The surface was still, but the current ran fast below.

The stillness, the quietness actually terrified me.

This was the most dramatic moment of my young life, and there was no drama!

There should have been clapping thunder, torrents of rain, and steepling waves lashing at our vessel, as a physical embodiment of my inner storm. But there was none.

Just stillness, silence, and an old man rowing a boat.

I looked at our rower now. Despite his strong build, he had a gentleness in his eyes that suggested his inner fortitude would protect you more than his enormous frame would harm you.

He held the oars in long, slender hands that had a grace I hadn't seen, and when he gestured it was as though he could carve the air with every movement.

The longer he rowed, however, the lighter his grip became as he visibly tired. I was in no hurry to reach our destination and our destiny therein, but I felt compelled to help.

'May I take a turn at rowing?' I enquired, with unusual diplomacy for me.

'That is a kind offer, young man. Have you rowed before?'

'A little. There was a pond in our village where I fished in the summer.'

'Good, good! Maybe one day I shall take you boating, with your grandfather's permission, but I feel he would prefer me to assume command of the vessel on this voyage!'

'Okay.'

'Please forgive my clunking oarsmanship, young sir. I'm not as strong as once I was!' He smiled and for the first time on that strange day, I felt a modicum of warmth and the storm inside me lulled for a moment.

As it did so, there I saw it, towering in black majesty through the fog.

We had arrived at Kerioth.

PART TWO

My Grandfather's Clock

FOURTEEN

LUCY WAS BORN SIX MINUTES BEFORE ME.

Why tell you this now, you ask? Especially as the story is just getting interesting, or at least I hope it is getting interesting!

Well, those six minutes really ought not to have made a great deal of difference, but they did.

Lucy was very much my senior in every respect. I relied on her to lead me, and she relied on me to follow. I looked to my sister for guidance, and I always got it.

I miss her very much.

However, as we disembarked from our maiden voyage across the lake that day, I was the leader.

The events of the day had shaken her normal calm and assured exterior, and for the first time I saw my sister as a frightened little girl.

She had uttered not a word on our trip across the lake, and now as I took her hand to help her step off the craft, she didn't even look at me, she just stared blankly ahead like a sleepwalker.

'Lucy?'

'What?' she replied impatiently.

'Are you all right? I mean, you're very quiet.'

'I can't talk now. Not here. I feel like we're being watched.'

As I looked up at the battlements to which she pointed her gaze, I understood what she meant. It was as though a thousand spectres kept guard there, looking down on us upon that little jetty, lost souls of the fallen keeping a silent watch over that mausoleum of a house.

I understood about ghosts. I knew they were quite real. The unresting spirits of the dead trapped between the world of men and the Kaharian. Tibbs had told me all about them, but I'd never really sensed one until now.

Lucy and I used to play in the graveyard in the village all the time, jumping out on old ladies from behind cold stone tombs as they took the short cut back from the post office.

They didn't much like that! I distinctly remember coming home one day to see Tibbs deep in discussion with Miss Harrington (a moody old sow if ever there was one!) and the latter scolding Tibbs for letting us run wild, and filling our heads with nonsense about ghosts and spirits.

There were some people in the village who thought Tibbs was quite mad and even called her a witch for some of the strange things she could do.

I was never privy to those strange things. Like so much of my childhood, it was a bit of a mystery!

However, to a pair of twelve-year-old orphans the idea of the dead being able to live as ghosts didn't seem ghoulish at all. In fact, it was the only hope of seeing our parents we had.

Here in this place, though, while I could not see them with my eyes, I could sense their presence in my soul.

Terrible, sad thoughts went through my mind as my soul connected with these lost spirits. They seemed to reach within me, as if draining the energy from me so that they might live again.

'Keep your mind focused on the present.' Picardo's voice awoke me from my reverie, surprising in its firmness. 'These spectres will sap you of your life-force if you dwell on memory. Come quickly inside the castle, they cannot enter there.'

'Why do these ghosts guard the castle walls?' Lucy piped up.

'They are the souls of the damned, who fell during...'

'During what?'

Picardo hesitated: 'During... "the unpleasantness".'

Lucy continued her questioning: 'What unpleasantness? What happened?'

'I have said too much. Your grandfather will tell you more, I am sure, when the need arises.'

'When the need arises? Maybe I need to know now!'

'I am sorry Miss Lucia. I have no place to discuss this further. All will become clear, I am quite sure.'

The old man swiftly guided us through a small oak doorway into a dusty corridor. It was an un-grand entrance to this grand castle, but we were inside and seemingly safe from the terrors that lurked on the castle walls and seemed to frighten even old Picardo.

So, this was it: the moment we would meet our one surviving relative. The one final link to the past we hadn't known. Yet my mind was not filled with questions about our history at that moment, but more of the future and what it held, and those questions filled me with fear previously unimagined.

Picardo fired up a gas lamp and we made our way along the stone passageway. The cold of the damp floor permeated through our shoes and the smell of stagnant water infiltrated the air.

'This way, please.' We helplessly followed the servant as he led us down the dank walkway. We reached the end without any further horror and Picardo threw open a heavy wooden door at the end of the passage.

Light!

That was the overwhelming, and surprising, sensation that greeted us from the room beyond.

Our eyes had become so accustomed to the gloom that seemed to surround Kerioth, and indeed, our fate, that we had to shield our eyes from the brightness ahead.

We walked out into what was the grandest room either of us had, and to this day have, seen. The dazzling light was that of a thousand candles, shimmering from their perches on crystal chandeliers and ornate candelabrae; the walls were hung with richly woven rugs from the east and beautifully embroidered tapestries. At the centre stood a curving, marble staircase, the balustrade clothed in gold-leaf.

It was as opulent as it was beautiful. As impressive as it was oppressive.

'Our grandfather owns all this?' I stumbled as I surveyed the scene in total awe.

'He does. It is amazing, the treasures that fear can buy.'

'What do you mean?'

'For all his greatness and intellect, not all your grandfather's dealings could be described as honest or even-handed. "Ill-gotten gains" is, I think, the phrase they use. I'm sorry, Master Joshua, I've said too much…'

'Yes, you have!' a tremulous voice quaked from the top of the staircase. The owner of the voice was still unseen, hidden behind a magnificent balustrade with a golden bear at its peak.

'My Lord, forgive me, I…'

'No matter, Picardo. The children will soon learn all there is to know. I will spare no detail.' The disembodied voice started to make its way down the stairs. The vocalist remained unseen but his footsteps were heavy and fearful. 'Oh yes, they will soon know everything. Things that their harridan of a schoolmistress never dared to share with them, in order to save the little dears' anguish! Ha! What of my anguish? Well, soon they will know! Children, welcome to Kerioth!'

As if from nowhere, he appeared from behind the heavily gilded stair rail just feet away from us.

Lucy gave an audible gasp and I recoiled as I looked on at the man I knew to be our grandfather.

'More monstrous than you dared believe, eh? More hideous than the beasts of your worst nightmares? Ha! Behold me! Do I disgust you? Do I?'

The question was met with shocked (and disgusted) silence.

'Well, you disgust me, you vile little creatures with your perfect smiles and your golden hair. Pah! To me you are ugly little maggots! How dare you turn your heads and shy away from me!'

'Master, may I advise a modicum of civility… if you want the children to do as they are bidden.'

'The children will do as they are told, Picardo. As with all who have served me, they will do so for one reason and one alone. Not love. Not respect. Not duty. But fear! They will be too terrified not to cede to my every wish! Now get them out of those foul rags, wash them and bring them to the drawing room, where their true education toward their calling shall begin.'

With that the old man disappeared through a door, slamming it behind him.

Looking back, it was a theatrical entrance with but one intent: to strike unbounded fear into our hearts. He succeeded in his aim, and we were transfixed by his horrible power.

We were so overwhelmed by his hideous appearance and terrifying oratory that we barely noticed the old man's wheezing and his reliance on a walking stick.

As Picardo led us to our quarters, in our minds the daemon's physical fragility was a distant second to the feeling of absolute dread in our hearts at what was in store.

He had won the first battle. Fear was his weapon, and fear had struck us dumb.

Fifteen

THERE HAVE BEEN TIMES, looking back, when I wondered whether this could have been the moment to run from that place. Overpower the decrepit servant, take the boat and head for land. There was a village not far away, where surely there would be shelter, or at least horses that would carry us to safety.

Yet as I removed the ridiculous undersized clothes that Tibbs had dressed me in what seemed like a lifetime ago, and stared into the flames of a log fire in the room Lucy and I were to share, escape never even entered my mind.

Why?

A get-away plan should have been hatching at that moment, yet something stopped it. Was it fear? Was it resignation to a dreadful fate? Or was it faith?

Tibbs had brought us up to believe in something, though she never named it, but told us when we needed it, and when we were ready to hear its call, it would speak to us.

'Submit your will, and you will not fall,' she had told us.

For some reason, as I recounted her words, standing, listening to the crackle of the fire, I felt no urge to flee, but instead compelled to stay and trust it would all be all right.

I had no way of knowing, of course, if it would all be all right, but I have come to know that that is what faith is! Putting your trust into something you cannot see, cannot hear, cannot touch.

I listened, as Tibbs had bid me do, and I heard nothing.

Maybe there was nothing there, or maybe I just wasn't ready to hear.

'We don't have a choice, do we?' Lucy asked, trembling, as she stood in the firelight in her new, beautifully tailored, but plain brown dress.

'Actually, I think we do!'

'What! How can we? We're trapped here.'

'We're not though, are we? It would be easy to escape. They're both old men, we'd out-muscle and outrun them both, but I don't think we're meant to.'

'How do you mean?'

'I think there's a purpose to us being here, and it's not just to pander to the whims of an aging monster. I think there is a purpose for us, too.'

'You're not making any sense.'

'I know, I know. Just trust me. I don't have any answers yet, but I think we will have them soon. And as you said to me, we may find out who we are and where we have come from, about our parents.'

'Okay. I trust you.'

'Good. Whatever happens, Lucy, we must stick together. That's our best, our only hope in this.'

'I'm right beside you. Well maybe a step or two behind... you can go first!'

'Chicken!'

And for the first time in about twelve chapters of this chronicle, we smiled!

Sixteen

THE CASTLE AT KERIOTH, despite its vast scale, was surprisingly easy to navigate.

The main rooms of the building were located in the circular keep, and for the most part the rooms opened onto the central hallway that we had first entered.

So Lucy and I made our way unguided to meet with our grandfather, out of our room, round the balcony, down the magnificent marble staircase, and beyond the ornately carved door that he had slammed dramatically behind him to terminate our first meeting.

We trod our path slowly and cautiously. What we anticipated might happen, I am none too sure, but we made our way down and found ourselves at the doorway.

'Ready?' I asked of Lucy.

'No!' she sighed.

'Oh, well!' I rapped firmly at the door.

There was a grunt from within, which I took as a signal to enter, and I swung the cumbersome door open.

The room was lit by a roaring fire at the end of an elongated elliptical chamber. By the fireside, a good sixty feet away, was a single armchair, the back toward the door. It was silhouetted against the firelight, and we saw its occupant lean sinuously forward to poke the fire.

'Come forth!' the man in the chair summoned.

I myself summoned what courage I had to take my first trembling step toward the fire, but as my shoe touched surely down on the lushly carpeted floor, I started to allay what trepidation I had and walked on.

In describing my grandfather as monstrous previously, I gave you little to go on by way of physical description.

What was most monstrous was that in many ways he was quite normal. He was tall, strongly built, with a bearing of authority and grace, despite his age. But his face! Monstrous!

Like an overdone beef steak left out in the sun, his skin was dried out to leathery, sinewy cragginess. His sunken eye-sockets were like maggot holes and where a mane of hair perhaps once proudly grew, there were now just a few wispy strands, topped with the trademark of his fall from grace: two small but clearly defined horns.

As we approached now, that devilish outline was black against the bright fire glow.

Suddenly, from the shadows Picardo stepped forward, startling Lucy and me alike.

Our gasp in turn startled our grandfather, as he dropped the poker into the fire and muttered some unfathomable curse.

'Miss Lucia, Master Joshua,' the servant greeted us, 'may I bring you some refreshment? Perhaps a little something to eat?'

'Good grief, man! Let them settle! I know we have not done much entertaining these many years, but you seem to have lost all sense of etiquette! Children, forgive my overzealous servant. We are really most anxious that you are comfortable here.'

'Umm... well, thank you,' Lucy offered in a somewhat uncomprehending gratitude.

The horrifying creature who had scared us into horrified silence barely an hour earlier was now our most genial host. Charming, eloquent and delightful.

I am not sure which was more frightening!

WITH AN INSISTENT GESTURE from his spidery fingers we were ushered onto a long upholstered stool opposite his own imposing leather armchair.

'I am rather afraid I didn't make the best impression when I greeted you earlier, children, for which I really must apologise. I have lived for many years alone, and may have come across as a little – how can I put it? – brusque, perhaps?'

We uttered not a word, like tongueless dolts. The great orator continued: 'I don't know where to begin. Honestly, I don't. All these many wasted years and now I leave it until the light is fading before I look upon you, my own flesh and blood. Can you forgive a foolish old man his folly?'

Lucy gulped, took a deep breath, and then, in little more than a whisper: 'I'd like to know why we are here, now.'

'Dear Lucia, so you shall presently.'

'I'd like to know now, sir.' Normally I was the impetuous one, but Lucy was steely and sure as she spoke this time.

'Sir? Dear child, there is no need for such formality here. We are family. One flesh. I am your grandfather, dear. What shall it be? Grandad? Grampy? Pops?'

The nicer he tried to be, the more ghastly he appeared in my eyes.

'I'd prefer to stick to "sir", if it's all the same.'

Lucy's impetuousness had become impertinence and he didn't like it. He didn't like it at all, and just for a second the mask of friendliness slipped as he looked Lucy up and down before fixing her with a glaze from his dead, black eyes.

'Very well, if that is what you prefer. I understand this situation may take some adjustment. I hope that I shall earn your respect and with it the honour of having you address me as your own kin.'

'Thank you for respecting my wishes.'

The beauty of my sister was her very great sincerity and dignity. Even at the age of twelve, she had managed to score the opening point against a devious and experienced opponent. She was a marvel to have as an ally! And a nightmare to have an argument with!

'Of course you are right, as well, Lucy. You do deserve some explanation. Let me be honest with you children. I am not as other men. Not like the men you will have seen chopping wood, or milking cows in that dreary little backwater of yours. Not even like Picardo.'

He hesitated, or at least feigned hesitation to build the drama: 'You see, the world you know is not all there is. I was born into the world of spirits. I was created not in this realm, of flesh and blood as you were, but of an ethereal essence.'

'Are we meant to understand this?'

'I am a daemon!' the old man eventually spat out, 'Is that plain enough for you?'

'A daemon? You mean a bad spirit? Like the imps?'

'No, not like the imps! Did that woman teach you nothing?'

The old man was fighting hard now to maintain his veneer of calm. 'This is perhaps a complex subject, children. It has been a long and emotional day for all of us. I suggest we get some rest and talk more over breakfast. Picardo keeps a small farm on the estate. There will be fresh milk and eggs. Now I bid you goodnight.'

With that he stood and just walked out.

Picardo entered with a tray: 'I have brought you some tea and toast. Am I to assume the master has retired to his cot for the evening?'

'What is a daemon, Picardo?' I asked.

'Oh, Master Joshua. You ask me of things that are beyond my comprehension, of a world that is above my humble understanding. One of the principal rules of domestic service is to ask few, if any, questions of those you serve. So it is with my master.

'You will learn all you wish to learn. I am sure of that, young ones. Now, who is for tea?'

Seventeen

DESPITE THE MILLION THOUGHTS swimming around my mind that night, I soon found myself in the land of nod.

Our quarters were more than comfortable. The bed soft, the duvet downy and warm. In other circumstances, it might have made a very happy home.

The warm tea and buttery toast had beaten away hunger, but also some of the butterflies and nervous energy that had built up throughout the day.

Lucy and I barely spoke as we climbed into fresh pyjamas and then the fresh linen of the bed sheets. Too full, too tired to think or speak any more, we slept.

And we remained sleeping until the small hours of the morning, when I was suddenly awakened by a sound at the window.

A soft, but audible scratching sound.

'Lucy! Lucy! Are you awake?'

There was no reply, so I assumed she was not.

First, I thought of the spirits we had sensed on our arrival at the castle.

Do lost souls scratch at windows?

There was only one way to find out, so I silently removed myself from the sheets, swung my legs out from the covers, and tucked my feet into the slippers neatly stowed at the side of my bed.

Moonlight shone through the light curtain at the window, and silhouetted there was the shape of whatever was making the noise.

Curiosity drew me closer to the window; my fear at what monster may lie beyond was consumed by my boyish need to know.

I drew back the curtain.

'What the...?'

Lucy awoke. 'Josh? What are you doing? What is it?'

Before she could speak further, I had unfastened the window and lifted it open.

The creature leapt through the window, landing neatly on all fours before giving a familiar wiggle and brushing contentedly against my legs.

Lucy jumped up from her bed. 'Astrador!'

Our feline friend purred as Lucy scooped him from the ground into her embrace.

'He must have climbed onto the back of the carriage as we rode off. Oh, you clever, clever cat!'

How Astrador did get there would, of course, remain a mystery as, being a cat, he wasn't particularly talkative, but as we pulled all the bedding onto the floor to set up a makeshift bed for the three of us, he was a most welcome companion that night.

I went back to sleep to the sound of gentle purring and slept a dreamless sleep until daybreak and the morning star appeared in the east.

DAY BROKE THROUGH THE OPEN CURTAIN in our room. I awakened and gently removed the moggy that lay on top of me, awake, alert, as if he were a sentinel keeping guard over my sister and me.

I went to the window and saw the most stunning view. The sun glistened off the gentle ripples of the surface of the lake and set behind it were those black mountains of the previous evening's journey, brilliantly transformed to crimson as the baked red clay shone in the sun's glare.

Lucy stirred as I got myself dressed and smiled as she woke.

'Morning!'

'Morning! It is so beautiful outside.'

'That may be. But we have an appointment inside if you will recall.'

We dressed in awkward silence and made our way down the central staircase.

At the foot of the stairs stood an imposing mahogany grandfather clock, which seemed rather appropriate in my grandfather's house!

The mechanism must have been broken because it was running slow and every now and then it would jam and then spring forwards a couple of seconds.

The poor thing had seen better days.

We made our way into the magnificent dining room where Picardo had told us to attend for breakfast, but there was no-one there, and so we did as most hungry children do, and followed our noses.

The kitchen door was ajar and as well as the delightful smell of fresh bread, there was the distinct sound of singing.

We pushed the door further open to be confronted with the most surprising sight! For the singing chef was not the servant Picardo, but our grandfather.

'Ah, children! Children! Come, be seated. I thought we'd break our fast in the informality of the kitchen this morning. Much more relaxing than that stuffy old banqueting room. I hope you will indulge me. I thought I would cook this morning; Picardo is making some other preparations for me. I do not have much call for cooking when I have a servant, but it really is most agreeable. I hope the fare will be up to scratch for you.'

'I am sure it will be fine,' I reassured in bewildered amusement at the sight of the old devil in an apron.

'I do hope you like scrambled eggs. It's my favourite, and if I am being wholly honest, it is one of the few things I can cook!'

'Scrambled eggs would be lovely. Thank you.'

'Now, Picardo baked some bread before he left, so help yourselves, it really is rather good, and there is also a fresh pot of coffee, so please do tuck in. There's some blackberry jam too. Picardo makes it himself and most excellent it is.'

'Thank you,' I said as I cut myself a slice of bread, smothered it in the deliciously thick conserve and gorged myself on its gooey goodness.

With mouth half-full, I blurted, 'That's really, really good!' Lucy just looked at me, appalled at my table-manners, or lack of them.

'Now, it is such a bright, sunny day, I thought you might like to have some time to yourselves to go for a walk around the island.'

'The island?' I knew we had crossed a lake, but had not realised that we were at the centre of it.

'Oh yes. The castle is on an island in a huge, tidal lake. We are a good three mile swim from the nearest land. Not that I can swim. Once maybe, but not now. Still, despite our remoteness, there is plenty of scope for exploration on the island: beaches, cliffs, caves. Although I would urge you not to go into the caves...'

'The lost spirits?' Lucy said.

'You are quite safe in the daylight, but the lost spirits live off the darkness. They live in the caves by day and venture out at night, looking for something. Who can tell what?'

'Sir? You said last night about the world of spirits, what did you mean?'

'Oh, let's not talk of such things now. There will be plenty of time for talk later. Now, scrambled egg all round!'

And so we ate up a delicious and convivial breakfast in anticipation of journeying out onto the green expanses of Kerioth Island.

WE SWUNG OPEN THE KITCHEN DOOR and galloped out onto a set of stone steps. We bounded up in twos to reach the glorious sunlight we could see shining above, and at the top were greeted by the most glorious vista of my young life.

This side of the castle had a manicured stretch of lawn which seemed to just drop into the stunning blue of open sea. In the far distance could be made out a rocky coastline, presumably the mainland from which we had come.

We careered across the lawn to get a better look. The lawn did, as we thought, just drop into the ocean, for it terminated at the top of a cliff; a few rugged, jagged rocks were the only relief from an otherwise sheer drop.

A hundred feet below, the rough waves smashed against the foot of the cliff, rumbling like the distant growl of thunder and sending a cloud of fine spray high into the air.

We followed a pathway from the top of the cliff banking down the right of the lawn. We didn't know where it led, but it led downhill, and downhill meant closer to the water, which is where we wanted to be.

It was funny that despite all the anxiety of the last day and the hundreds of miles that separated us from the place we lived and loved, the adventure and freedom we felt that morning felt very much like being at home.

We hiked excitedly down the rocky path that had been roughly hewn from the footfall of many years; we also noticed on the path the cloven hoof-prints of what we took to be animal tracks, at the time. Their significance was quite lost on us.

The path became steeper as we ventured back and forth in zig-zags toward sea level, and we stepped carefully, placing one sideways foot at a time, using a hand against the red clay to steady ourselves.

The sound of lapping waves grew ever closer as the path began to flatten out and we found ourselves running toward a small beach of immaculate golden sand, each grain kissed by the light of the autumn sun.

We had managed to reach this stage of our lives without ever seeing a beach before. Home was a land-locked sort of place. The pond where Farmer Jessop kept his fish stocks and where we were sometimes allowed to boat in summer (and sometimes not allowed, but did so anyway) was the only expanse of water we'd seen bigger than a bathtub.

What stared back at us now was something altogether different. It was vast! The sea seemed to extend forever, as though if you swam to the edge you would fall off the face of the earth.

Any thoughts we may have harboured of escape probably vanished in that moment – swimming wasn't either of our strongest suits. In fact we had learnt to swim only out of the fact that our quarrels normally resulted in the rowing boat capsizing on the pond and us both taking a good drenching!

However, at that particular moment, escape wasn't high in our thoughts. If we didn't think too much, we had merely swapped one paradise for another, and now we had a whole new environment to explore and make mischief in. The nefarious motives of an old daemon could not have been further from our thoughts.

The little beach was surrounded by steep cliffs, in what I now know to be a cove. (Tibb's geology books hadn't taught me that, or if they had, I hadn't learnt it!)

We soon found, too, that where the sand was damp it could be shaped into forms. With a couple of hours' toil, we managed to build a model of the castle out of sand! Yes, I know, you've all done it, but that morning Lucy and I were pioneers in our new world, and the castle of sand was a breakthrough of staggering proportions!

We sat back in satisfaction at our accomplishment, looking out at the beauty and power of the constant crashing of the waves against the rocks further up the coast, when we saw a familiar figure in the distance, clanking and spluttering his way to shore on his old boat.

We leapt to our feet. 'Picardo! Picardo! Over here!'

The old servant looked over his shoulder from his seat in the ancient craft and looked alarmed, changing course to head for the beach where we stood.

As the vessel came into shallow water, he leapt (well, as much as a frail old man could) from the boat into the ankle-deep briny and rounded on us sharply: 'What are you doing here? You must get back to the castle now! You cannot leave this place!'

'Our grandfather told us to go out and play, to roam the island freely,' Lucy protested.

'He did?'

'Yes, he did.' The old man was clearly startled by this turn of events. 'We are not escaping, Picardo. Look, we even made a model castle in the sand!'

He was flummoxed: 'Well, I... well, I suppose that's all right then. Forgive me, I just expected, just expected Lord Aquila to want to be close to you today, catching up and such like.'

'Oh no!' Lucy exclaimed looking toward our sandy masterpiece. 'It is being washed away by the sea. It will disappear in a few minutes – quickly, let's dig a trench to stop the water.'

'Leave it be,' Picardo restrained her, 'let it go the way of all things. What is built on sand is destined to crumble and fall. You cannot stop the motion of the tide more than you can the relentlessly ticking clock. If only your grandfather would see that. Nothing lasts forever.'

'What was that?'

'Nothing, miss. Nothing you won't come to understand.'

'I do wish you wouldn't talk in riddles,' Lucy said.

Picardo laughed. 'You have a wise head on those shoulders, Miss Lucy. I am quite sure these riddles, and many greater ones, you will unravel before long. Now, how about I row you round to the other side of the island and you can help me carry these provisions inside. You can build another castle tomorrow.

'In fact, Master Joshua, you mentioned that you were something of an oarsman...'

'I certainly try...'

'Well, it's a calm day, perhaps you'd care to be the captain on this voyage?'

With a spring in my step I clambered aboard and pushed away from our sandy harbour. A pleasant half an hour followed as Picardo navigated us round our beautiful rocky habitat. Majestic cliffs, craggy caves and archways where seabirds cooed and seal cubs basked in the late afternoon sun.

I guided us up to the little pier where we had first set foot on the island the night before and carried baskets of groceries up the stony path – fruit, vegetables, sausages and venison steaks the size of my face! Dinner that evening would be a sumptuous feast. We would need to be well fed for the adventures to come.

WHEN WE ARRIVED BACK AT THE CASTLE, our grandfather was waiting for us.

'Children! Welcome back! I trust you have had a good day.'

'Yes, thank you. We found a little beach and we played in the sand, and then Picardo found us and we went round the island on his boat...'

'A very full and active day by the sounds! You must be famished. Now go and draw a bath, you are covered in sand. You will find fresh clothes on your beds. Picardo and I will rustle up a banquet worthy of two such gallant explorers!'

'Thank you.' With that we rushed up the stairs. Our spirits had been lifted beyond measure by the day's events.

We had experienced a freedom and friendship we little expected in this place, and our apprehension was slowly ebbing away.

That was his plan, of course, to draw us to him, but at that time we had all but forgotten with whom we were dealing and that the reason for our being in Kerioth had yet to be explained.

All of that was about to change.

EIGHTEEN

'IS THERE ANY KETCHUP?' I asked expectantly.

He looked at me, genuinely horrified by my innocent enquiry.

'My dear boy! You are eating hand-reared pheasant, braised in its own stock and red wine sauce, then fried off in a jus of garden plums and seventy-year-old Napoleon brandy. If the Pidaja had known that people would one day smother every item they shoved in their ungrateful mouths in that red muck, he'd have never invented it.

'Enjoy the flavours, let them sit in your mouth. Let them tease your taste-buds. You have a lot to learn about the finer things in life, young man!'

I lowered my head in shame, as Lucy suppressed a giggle at my foolishness. I cut a slice of the meat on my plate and mopped some of the sauce before popping it in my mouth.

'Don't chew yet,' said my grandfather. 'Just let it sit for a second, then chew... slowly.'

I did as he said, fearing another lecture in fine dining if I failed to comply.

The sliver of pheasant breast sat on my tongue. The flavours were overwhelming, it just oozed goodness. First the honeyed sweetness of the sauce and then a second kick as the smokiness of the meat swirled on my palette.

I began to chew, and with each bite, a fresh wave of flavour and aroma struck me.

I swallowed down.

'My goodness. You were right! It's fantastic!' I said as I hurriedly carved another piece.

'Slowly!' he implored, 'Savour every bite, every flavour, as though it were the last thing you would ever eat.'

The banquet was sumptuous as we ravished a table laden with game, sweet potatoes, and fresh beans and carrots from the garden. Washed down with cherry cordial and the lightest, lightest coffee mousse. I swore that from then on I would never allow tomato ketchup to pass my lips. A promise that I am proud to say I have kept to this day.

Exhausted by gluttony we sat back in our chairs, our full stomachs sated in every way.

'Shall we retire to the sitting room?' grandfather asked, standing as he did so.

Lucy and I lifted our weary and bloated bodies from the dining room and walked through to collapse onto a comfy sofa.

Our grandfather stood at the fireside, gently stoking the flames. He spoke: 'I am so pleased you children could join me here at Kerioth. I know I have been absent from your lives until now, and I am sorry for that, and I am sorry that I have waited until now to know you, especially since I am soon to die.'

From our semi-slumber we both straightened at these words, and watched and listened spellbound as he continued.

He removed a pocket watch from his waistcoat and dangled it in front of our eyes like the fairground hypnotist we had once seen on a visit to the big town.

'This, you see, is what is making my light fade.'

The second hand of the golden timepiece faltered in its constancy and occasionally skipped a beat, sometimes stopped completely before heading off again on its circular route.

'You know, of course, that I am a daemon. But do you know what that means?'

Lucy cleared her throat, her voice sounded tired, almost distant, almost drunk: 'I think so. Tibbs used to call us little daemons if we were naughty. It is a bad spirit.'

He laughed a horrible laugh. 'A bad spirit! Hahaha! The old woman really did want to hide you from the reality, the dreadful reality of your lives, didn't she?'

His words were beginning to bite now.

'Bad spirit! Oh no, it's much worse than that.'

I felt a haze come over me as though this was all a feverish dream. Maybe the brandy jus had gone to my head, as it now began to throb with every intense word he spoke. Ideas, realms, secrets I barely had the wit or capacity to understand.

'Every pained tick of that watch, children, brings me closer to death. Every faltering stroke, my heart grows a little weaker. That watch is my life; when it stops, it is over. I will be no more. Death is inevitable. Unless...'

Our eyes were fixed on him.

'Children, I want to tell you a story.'

Nineteen

'REMIND ME, LUCY, JOSHUA, how old are you now?'

I spoke first, head still banging: 'Twelve. We're both twelve.'

'Yes, that's right. Twelve years old. Have you any idea how old I might be? Don't be shy now, I won't be offended in the least if you guess wrong.'

Lucy, ever the methodical one, even in the brandy-haze, calculated: 'Well, our mother was twenty-five when we were born, if you were around the same when she was born, and we are now twelve, that would make you a little more than sixty.'

'Sixty! Lucy, you flatter me. Thank you!'

'Maybe seventy then.'

'It may surprise you, children, to know that my actual age is four thousand, five hundred and sixty-nine years.'

'What?' I said, staggered.

'That's not possible,' Lucy concluded.

'Not by any normal standards, my dear, no. But as you know, I am not a "normal" man. Now please, don't interrupt, and I will do my best to explain.

'Many thousands of years ago, there was no world. There was no sun, no moon, no light, no dark, no day, no night. Not even any tomato ketchup, Joshua!

'Then from nothing it was created, by a being greater than your young minds could begin to conceive. The great being could create anything, a mind brilliant enough to set the planets in orbit, to create every living thing. The grass in the fields, the water in the lake, the soil in which we grow our crops. And then when it had created all this, it sought fellowship in the tending of its infinite realm, and so created a legion of envoys to administer its work and see it done. They were called angels.

'Thus, I was created.'

He turned once more to the fire, and thrust the poker into the flames rhythmically as he spoke.

'Not, as you were, created of man and woman. No. I was created of that great mind from dust, and as things stand, that is to whence I will return before much longer.

'You have heard of angels, haven't you? That hag Tibbs, did give you some spiritual education?'

We both nodded, and Lucy, hesitating, spoke: 'I have seen pictures of angels in books. You don't look like them at all.'

'I did. Before my fall.'

'You fell? You were in an accident?'

'I fell from grace. Not physically... I had wings, after all! Ha! My fall, and that of my closest allies, was sudden, swift and devastating. Cuts and bruises heal, broken bones mend. Broken souls cannot.

'The great one, you see, was all-powerful and was not to be crossed. I crossed it and lost. Its retribution was expedient and executed without mercy. One day I was an angel, magnificent, beautiful and powerful. The next, I was a daemon – twisted, foul and crumbling.'

'What did you do to fall from grace?'

'You will assume, and I take it from your tone, Lucy, that I was at fault. You will learn, children, very soon in fact, that you face choices, temptation. Where there is choice, there is pain, and where there is choice you may be on the losing side. History is written by the victors, the moral high-ground is claimed by the triumphant. The losers are the unheard voices. The victorious have their statues and their monuments, the losers are banished. The victorious walk eternally in a crown of light, the losers are plunged into a darkness so black that your young minds would quiver at the horrors it holds.

'Tonight though, the losers will rise again, and history and the whole future of this realm will be written again.'

His rasping voice took on a fuller, deeper sound as he spoke these last words. He was a proud man, and it was clear that whatever it took, he was determined to right the wrong he felt had been done to him.

He took his pocket-watch from his waistcoat and surveyed it ponderously. His tone was more sombre than it was fearsome now: 'Time: such a cruel mistress. Seconds, minutes, hours, days, weeks and years. The most fateful and fatal word man ever created. Once I rejoiced that there was no time, and now I lament that I've no time left. Haha!' His sardonic chuckle was pitiful and painful.

I wanted to understand what was at work in that brilliant but twisted head of his, 'What do you mean? You say there was no time, but...'

He cut in, 'There was no time. Not in the beginning. When it created the heavens and the earth there were no divisions into day and night and years and decades. It just didn't exist. Everything was ageless, everything was immortal.

'Then foolish man with his quest for order and reason invented this,' he dangled the watch in front of my face, 'and killed his own brethren in so doing.

'With time, things became old, things aged, and with age came deterioration and decay. With deterioration and decay came destruction and death.'

'But surely this creator, this great mind you talk of, could change all that, if it wanted to?'

'Oh yes, Joshua, oh yes it could. But then what would it do with the likes of me? You see, for me, once time stood still. I was an angel. I was immortal and unaffected by the constraints of time and space. But when I stood and faced its fearful wrath, my wings were clipped and in their place was conjoined to my very soul this watch to be my constant companion, and constant reminder of my disgrace and my mortality. I became a prisoner of time, and this watch is the warden of my lingering death sentence.'

He held the watch in one hand, and with the other loosened his dressing robe and yanked his shirt from the waist of his trousers. He exposed just an inch or two of his blackened, wrinkled, pock-marked skin, but it was enough to see that the gold chain that the watch was joined to was not attached to any belt or button, but to my grandfather's naval.

'You see, just as you mortals are chained to your mothers at birth, so I am to mortality.'

He paused as he saw how he had shocked us into silence, and his mood softened.

'Another log for the fire, I think.'

He walked over to the hearth, and tossed a strip of timber into the flames. He absent-mindedly poked at it as he continued, 'You could never, in your wildest imaginings, comprehend the pain of the fallen. To have everything and to lose all.

'But perhaps you do know part of my pain. For you too have lost much, young ones, due to the spite of our malevolent creator.'

'I don't understand,' I stuttered, genuinely confused.

'Your parents...'

'...died in a boating accident...'

'...were murdered,' he cut me off. 'By the enemy, or by the enemy's brainwashed sheep and their blind prejudice.

'Your father, foolish, sentimental man, eleven winters past, made his way here to Kerioth to visit his fragile old father.

'But men of the creator are wicked – truly wicked. Your parents stopped at the inn on the mainland, and the barkeeper asked their business.

'Honest fool that he was, your father told the man that they were to visit his ailing father, Lord Aquila.

'The little men of the world are ignorant and prejudiced, children. Here, the village folk saw their chance to do some work for "good" and inflict pain on the old daemon, whose shadow bore down on their town these many years.

'Your parents were never seen again. Save for the bones that some dog scratched out of a shallow grave.

'They were murdered?' Lucy's voice trembled as realisation hit her.

'Yes, by "good" men, my dear. Men who celebrated their triumph over the daemon by holding a Mass of thanksgiving in their temple.'

Lucy's elegant poise crumbled, and her delicate frame curled, her shoulders silently, rhythmically moving up and down as she sobbed silently.

With tears in my eyes, but resolve in my heart, I spoke: 'Go on.'

My grandfather eyed me up and down before resuming his narrative.

'On your parents' death, I wished for you to come and be with me, to become your guardian, and to bring you up here. However, your Aunt Tibbs, not your real aunt as you know, usurped me, and with my health failing, I had not the strength nor the will to fight with her over such dear, precious children, and so I ceded your custody to her.'

'So why do you want us now? Why bring us here, away from our home? Tell us these shameful horrors of our past?' My temper, stirred by our situation and those horrors of which I spoke, stayed barely in check as I spewed forth my barrage of questions.

'Joshua, you are an astute boy: your mind unswerving from your focus, whatever distractions are laid in the path. You are all I hoped and needed you to be.'

'What do you mean?'

'Children, I am dying. In your earthly time, I have weeks, possibly only days left to walk this earth, and then... and then... *pfft.*' With this last he waved his spindly hand to the air, and a cloud of fine dust spread from his fingers, hanging in the air before falling deftly to the ground.

Lucy was now listening, her voice still tearful. 'We have no wish for that to happen, but I don't see what we can do to help. We can be here, and will remain with you until the end, if that is what you wish...'

'That's not what he wishes,' I interjected, 'there is something more.'

My grandfather chuckled, throwing back his head, and dramatically giving three or four hearty claps of applause. 'Joshua, you impress me more with each passing moment! Lucy, there is more, so much more that you can do. That you *will* do.'

His attention was suddenly distracted and he exclaimed, 'What the...' as a familiar friend brushed its small, sleek black frame against his legs. 'What is this creature doing here? Get it out!'

'Certainly not!' Lucy said, bending to scoop up the furry intruder. 'Astrador is our friend.'

'What did you say? What did you call it?'

My grandfather was visibly shocked at this seemingly harmless development; I almost thought his ticker would give up there and then.

'Astrador; and he's not an "it", he's a "he".'

Under his breath, the old devil muttered darkly, 'No, it cannot be! Of course not! Mere coincidence.'

He fixed his gaze on the cat, who returned his stare with the assurance and knowingness that only cats can.

'Very well, though hold onto him. I do not get on with cats, and this is not a petting zoo.'

Throughout the fuss, my mind had stayed clear. 'Then what is this place? What would you have us do?'

'Oh Joshua, dear boy. Just a small thing, and yet the very greatest thing of all time.

'You ask me what is this place? Let me explain. How do you think angels, and daemons for that matter, came into the world of men?'

'Asking a question is a strange way of explaining...'

'Touché, my boy!'

'But I should imagine the spirits are beyond the dimensions of the earth and enter not by physical means.'

'A clever answer, and maybe I underestimated your understanding of the spiritual realm, however, it is much more simple: they use the door.'

'WILL YOU TAKE A WALK of faith with me, children?' He did not wait for a reply as he stood from his chair, and without pause or hesitation walked into the fireplace.

There was a gust and a flash of light, and Lucy screamed as the old man stepped into the flames.

And then stillness.

Lucy and I looked at each other in stunned disbelief at the impossibility we had just witnessed. Then in an instant, Astrador clawed at Lucy's arm, causing Lucy to drop him, and in one feline leap threw himself onto the fire.

'Astrador, no!' Lucy cried out, but it was too late. He had gone in a gust of wind and a flash of light.

Stillness came again, only a gentle lapping of flames and Lucy's tears breaking the silence. She knelt, weeping, two or three metres from the fire, as I inspected the scene.

'It cannot be. Lucy, I know this sounds crazy, but you don't suppose this fireplace is some kind of doorway?'

'I am not going in there, Josh,' she yelled at me, 'we will die.'

'Lucy. I do not think we will die. What would be the point of our grandfather's bringing us here and his long speeches on life and death if he merely meant to throw himself on the fire and end it all? The way Astrador followed also. Cats are smart, Lucy, especially Asti. I think this is the walk of faith grandfather mentioned and the doorway to the world of spirits.'

Lucy looked at me disbelievingly, and I grabbed her firmly round the waist and started to pull her toward the fire.

'Josh, what are you doing? Get off me! Get off me!' she said trying to wriggle herself free.

'Lucy, just trust me, please,' I said tightening my grip, but she was having none of it, and evaded my grasp.

'No Josh! I am sorry, I am not going to just walk into a fire. It will kill us both.'

I paused. 'All right, I understand... and I'm sorry.'

And with that I walked into the inferno, leaving my sister behind.

It was not in the least how I imagined. I felt the lick of the flames at my feet, but their touch was as sheets of silk, and within a couple of steps, I found myself free of them and a blast of cool air encouraged me to open my tightly closed eyes.

Again, the place I was now in was not how I imagined. In fact, it looked very much like I was still in the castle rather than another world.

My grandfather stood smiling at me, and he spoke first: 'You look bewildered, dear boy!'

'I am a little. This doesn't seem to be another world – the world of spirits you said was through a door.'

'Hahaha! Oh, dear Joshua, we have not entered that place. I cannot enter that place. We are merely in another part of the castle. I am sorry for my dramatic exit, but it served two purposes. The first was to test your faith – were you willing to take a risk to find out more – and you did not let me down, my boy. Secondly, to teach you a lesson, that things are not always what they seem, a lesson which will hold you in good stead in the coming hours and days. The fire is not always dangerous, the righteous mannered are not always agents of good, and the monstrous are not always monsters.'

Suddenly, I heard crying on the other side of the fire. It was Lucy. I turned back to the fire and shouted into the flame.

'Lucy! It's fine. I am safe! I made it to the other side. Just close your eyes and walk. Trust me.'

Ten seconds later, she was by my side, although it was clear that she had been beside herself with anguish in my momentary absence.

I noticed for the first time how tired she looked, and how this whole affair was draining the colour from her. Her eyes, which normally burned so bright, looked sunken, and her cheeks were tear-stained, as though dashed with rain.

Astrador came now to her side, and brushed his flank by her leg. She raised half a smile.

The atmosphere in the room seemed to change, and as I looked up at my grandfather, I saw his gaze was diverted over our heads. I turned sharply to see two newcomers to the assembly.

One, the friendly manservant, Picardo, was not unwelcome, but the other, who was already known to us, most certainly was.

'What are you doing here?' I spat at Innocent Quibble.

The lawyer gave that smug little bow of his, and smirked as he walked around us to my grandfather's side.

My grandfather spoke: 'I have asked Mr. Quibble to join us, as I have a task for him of great import. Remember, Joshua, how I told you that things are not always as they appear. Do not let Mr. Quibble's unfortunate appearance cause you to think ill of him.'

'It is his unfortunate and foul manner and character that make me think ill of him, sir.'

'Hold your tongue, Joshua.' The old devil's tone was sharp and clipped. Whatever my feelings about the loathsome toad, I would be advised to keep a civil tongue within my grandfather's earshot.

'What you did, both of you, in walking through the fire was a leap of faith. Faith will carry you a long way in what I am to ask of you. Tell me; do you believe the things I have told you?'

Given my earlier rebuke, I was too frightened to give any other answer. 'Yes, of course.'

'Then you are a fool! I am a daemon, boy! Sometimes I lie. Sometimes I tell the truth. My art is to mix the two together, truth and falsehood, until I create a world where no-one can truly remember what was true and what was a lie. That is why your parents' pitiful lives ended so tragically young... although that may also be a lie. You can never tell with me!

'However, what I have told you about myself, that I am a daemon, that I was an angel, and that very shortly I shall die, all of that, regrettably, is true, unless...'

'Unless...' I urged him.

'Unless you can do that which I am unable to do.'

Lucy, still disorientated, found strength to speak. 'Is this the place of which you spoke?'

'Goodness, no! Though I should like that it were, but, alas, I am banished from that place. My stepping even one foot into that most beautiful and damned of realms would see forces so terrific unleashed that your poor mortal eyes could not stand the sight.

'No, I cannot enter that place' – the pause in his melodramatic speech hung as heavily in the air as a leaden raincloud about to launch its unholy deluge – 'but you can.'

His words, although inevitable, cut through me like a knife. I wanted to pick Lucy up and run far from this place, but something in my heart intervened to the point where I heard myself speak; I heard my own voice, but the words were not mine.

'What must I do?'

The old man smiled his devilish smile.

For the first time I could see that maybe once he had been really quite handsome. There was a light in his eyes. It was the light of hope, missing before, but now burning again.

He did not speak in response to my question, but continued to smile as he walked down the length of the room to a set of wooden double doors at the far end.

As he walked away, the solicitor, Quibble spoke to me: 'This is the Átjaró chamber, a gateway.'

Lucy's ears pricked up: 'A gateway to... the Kaharian?'

My grandfather continued to walk away, but spoke now: 'Men had thought the way was closed, that only death could allow the spirit to find that place. But men are fools and have neither the wisdom nor the faith to walk through fire and water.'

He stood still with his back to us. The lumps on his back were prominent, the stumps of his dismembered wings. Then he made off again toward the doors, his stride showed a renewed vigour, a renewed life.

He reached the doors at the end of the room, pausing; his hands trembled as he caressed the carved wooden panels. With unnatural strength he flung the doors open. They flew from their hinges with the force of his thrust, spiralling through the air and into the lake beyond.

He stood there now, facing us, some distance away, but his eyes were ablaze.

'This is the place where you must show your faith. Pay your debt and give life to him from whom your lives sprang.'

Beyond the doorway stood the most spectacular vista. Water sprang from everywhere in a fine mist, and suspended magically above the lake, a stone ring... no, not a ring, a clock face! The numbers marked out I to XII. The lake's surface was turbulent but for the stretch leading to the giant stone clock which was as calm as a mill pond.

And then, something I could scarcely believe... my father! As clear as anything, he stood there, the man I could barely remember, and extended his hand to me.

Was this the portal? The gate to the Kaharian itself?

I started to make toward this most beauteous sight, my step purposeful, my intention resolute. I could at last meet my father! My mother! They were there, right ahead of me.

My trance was jolted by Lucy stepping in front of me.

'Get out of my way!' I cried.

'No, we don't know what this is!'

'Don't you see, this is the Kaharian! I want to go there!'

'No, it is the land of the dead.'

'Exactly! That is why I want to go! Don't you want to see our mother, or our father?'

'Josh. Not like this.'

I looked her squarely in the eye, and she returned my stare. With my resolve softened and the hypnosis, if that is what it was, broken, I turned to our grandfather.

'What do you want of us?'

He clapped his hands together in glee, like a child who had been promised ice cream every day of his life.

'Joshua, I want you to enter the Kaharian. I want you to find a box, and return it to me. That is all. No more. No less.'

'It will be dangerous. We are only children.'

'Not really. The Kaharian is full of angels and very kindly people. None will wish you any harm.'

'How can we trust you?'

'You cannot. And yet you must.'

'Why?' Lucy demanded.

'Children, when I die, there is no afterlife for me. I am damned. I will simply cease to exist, and everything I have begotten upon this earth will die with me. The carpet you stand on, the chair in the corner, this castle, even my own progeny.'

'You mean we will die with you?'

'Yes. Yes, I am rather afraid you will.'

I stepped forward now: 'What does this box contain?'

'Oh, not much; just a secret. A secret as old as time! Literally as old as time.' He chuckled in amusement at something he had said or thought. 'If you can do this thing for me, Joshua – and there will be two of you, so you will be quite safe – I can conjure the secret of eternal life! We only live and die because time runs out... but if there were no more time, that is to say, if time did not exist, as it was in the beginning, you will live, you two children, for ever!'

I was suddenly aware of Astrador at my trouser leg, clawing at the hem. I could have sworn his 'meow' sounded more like a warning 'neow', but I overlooked it.

'What does it look like, this box? Where will I find it?'

PART THREE

Thy Kingdom Come

Twenty

THERE ARE MOMENTS IN LIFE when you have a decision to make. Quite often neither of the choices is particularly appealing and yet, all the same, you must step one way or another.

On that fateful day, I remember it well, the choice was easy to make. Although the consequences of the choice scared me beyond imagining, I knew that going forward was the only way.

'Will we need to take anything? A map? Food? A weapon?'

'You will need only your wits and your faith. Trust your heart and instincts. They will be your guide, your nourishment and protection.'

I turned to my sister. 'Lucy, I will go first. Do not be afraid. I will be waiting on the other side for you. We can do this together; just as we have always done!'

'Josh, I am frightened. It could be a trap!'

'Lucy, trust me. I believe that whatever is happening to us here will come to good. Do you remember how Tibbs used to say, "It will all be alright in the end; and if it is not alright, it is not the end"?'

'I will see you on the other side.' She smiled hesitantly.

I stepped toward my grandfather. He laid his awkward, spindly hand on my shoulder.

'You will save a good many lives in doing this. Your actions will herald a new order in this world and the next.'

The waves of the lake thundered against the stone ring, but I heard not a sound. I looked out at the still path of water before me, toward the portal, a furlong ahead.

'How will I get there… the water… it is deep.'

'Why, how else? You walk!'

'But the water will…'

'Have faith, and step forward.'

I tentatively put the toes of my right foot toward the water, when suddenly, like a black shadow, Astrador flew past me, dancing over the surface of the water and into the centre of the stone ring.

There was a blinding flash of white light and a reverberating din, as though the souls of all the dead collectively drew breath; and he was gone.

I looked back to Lucy: 'Do they allow cats in the Kaharian?' I tried to joke.

'I imagine we are about to find out. Wait for me on the other side.'

'I will always wait for you. Be brave.' I squeezed her hand, and then let her go and turned back to the portal.

Again, I dipped my toe against the surface of the water. It broke the surface, but as I put the weight onto my foot, it did not submerge into the depths, but rested on the surface, the tiny ripples just tickling at my feet. I did the same with the left foot, and then the right in front of the left, and then the left in front of the right, and suddenly I knew I was walking on water. I had heard a legend that it could be done, but the tale had seemed impossible to my young ears.

So much had seemed impossible just a few short days ago. Dragged away from safety and seclusion to this ghostly castle, talk of daemons and angels, of immortality and the nature of time, walking on water, the Pidaja, and now I stood at the threshold of a place I thought I might only see when I died. If then.

Maybe I was going to die, maybe this was some devilish trick devised by my devilish grandfather to kill Lucy and me. And yet, though I trusted him not an iota, I trusted something, and so I stepped forward.

My step surely lasted but a second, and yet time moved past me at an unimaginable rate. I had seen the world move quickly before, on the swings or the merry-go-round in the playground, but this was something else. Like I had travelled from the dawn of time to the very end of days in just a moment. Visions of faces, places, familiar and unknown, flashed in front of me in a vortex of shapes, sounds and light; and then stillness. A sense of stillness and rest.

I had arrived.

Twenty One

I FIND IT HARD TO RECALL exactly my first impressions of a place I was to get to know well, but I think my overriding feeling was of isolation.

I stood in a field, which stretched as far as the eye could see in every direction. The portal through which I entered had no physical manifestation here and as I stepped back toward where I thought I had come from, no force grabbed me, and no entrance reappeared.

The landscape was flat. The field was just a dustbowl of dry mud, the colour and patina of ancient papyrus. The land was scorched by what I thought to be the sun, although its colour was, it seemed to me, a lilac hue. It seemed too cool a star to be the sun, but its heat beat down on the arid land nonetheless.

The only relief to the relentlessly golden-brown plain was a tree, maybe ten or a dozen furlongs off (so it seemed at the time).

Thus I was involved in taking in this place and the loneliness of being there, when it occurred to me that I shouldn't be alone – Lucy was still to come through!

By this stage, I had so disorientated myself by looking left and right and taking in this vast desert that I had completely forgotten where I had come from. I tried to realign myself to where I thought I had entered this realm. When I came through, I had been facing directly toward the tree, so if I now turned my back on it, then surely I would be looking back toward the portal.

So, I did so, and I stood and I waited.

Nothing.

I had yet to learn of the place they call the Kaharian that time and space are anything but constant, anything but absolute.

Having tired of standing in the unrelenting sunlight, I sat, for what seemed to me to be a period of three or four hours. Still facing toward the place where I thought I had emerged from the portal.

Nothing.

Sweat from the oppressive heat caked my flesh, and on my cheeks, the beads of perspiration mingled with salty tears.

I was quite alone, and I was quite afraid.

Where was Lucy? Where was Astrador, who had entered just minutes before me? Nowhere on the horizon had I seen the faintest trace of life.

I buried my head in my hands as I reconciled myself to the fact that I would surely die, when without warning I heard the words, 'Get up now, we have a way to travel before nightfall.'

'You? What are you doing here?'

The voice that had spoken was not the sweet tones of my sister as I was expecting, and when I turned to see the orator, I wished for the death I had desired in my loneliness.

'Your grandfather, wise man that he is, decided that you needed guidance on your all-important journey. A voice of experience to aid you in your quest.'

'Where is my sister?'

Innocent Quibble (for it was he) answered, 'My Lord thought that this assignment would be too arduous for your fragile sibling. He will take care of her, while I partner you. In any case, your grandfather is eager that you should return with the box post haste, and saw your sister's remaining with him as a potential incentive for you to complete your task.'

'I want to go back!'

'That is quite impossible, I am afraid, until...'

'I want to go back! I will show Lord Aquila that...'

But I didn't manage to finish the sentence before the blasted heath trembled beneath me.

'What is going on?'

'Do not speak his name! Do not even think his name! Your grandfather was exiled from here and even the thought of his name will stir the wrath of the Pidaja!'

'Even a thought will stir his wrath, his anger? How can he possibly know our thoughts?'

'He knows everything, sees everything and senses everything. He knows we are here, Joshua. Do not let the purpose of your mission be spoken of until the time is near.'

'You ask the impossible. The more I try to stop thinking about something, the more I will think of it.'

'Master Joshua, you simply must do as I say – your life depends on it.'

Twenty Two

THE ROOM ON THE LAKE had fallen quiet. The waters were still, and only the faint sobbing of a small girl curled in the corner broke the silence.

The old man sat upon a high-backed, carved wooden chair, soundlessly curling and uncurling his fingers around his cane.

Picardo the servant stood by, attentive and calm. If he had any inclination to go to help Lucy in her distress, he resisted it. His duty was, after all, to his master.

Faintly, from another room, a clock struck once upon the hour.

'Your tears will do you no good, child,' the wizened old creature spoke harshly, 'it is the only way to ensure your brother's return.'

Lucy, dishevelled and dirtied from lying on the dusty floorboards, unfurled herself and stood, her back straightened defiantly. 'Why wouldn't you let me go? Why bring me all this way and then leave me here?'

'My dear...'

'I am not your dear!' Lucy cut in.

'Very well. I never had any intention that you should both go to that place. What possible incentive would there be for you to return when you had experienced the beauty of the Kaharian? And, having never met you, how could I have possibly known which of the two would be brave and foolish enough to take the first step? This way is much neater. I take great delight in knowing that my propensity for scheming wickedness has not left me!'

'You are a monster!'

'How very observant of you! You'd just better hope it is not hereditary!'

Lucy's thoughts took another turn. 'Will he be safe? Joshua, I mean.'

'That rather depends...'

'Upon what?'

'Well, the Kaharian is for the vast majority the safest, most wonderful place of all the realms. It is an idyll, and calm and peaceful.'

There was inevitably going to be a 'but' coming soon.

'But, for those who enter with impure hearts or with motives that would denigrate the Kaharian, well...'

'Well?'

'A fury such as the earth has never seen and could never imagine will be released onto those poor souls.'

Tears welled again in Lucy's eyes. 'Oh, Josh...'

'And so you had better hope that your brother has no thought of heroism or trying to thwart my plans. He must simply retrieve the box, draw no attention, return it to me. You will have your brother back safely, I will have life again. Everyone goes home happy!'

'When Josh returns, you will let us go home? Home to Tibbs?'

'Oh, my dear girl. I am afraid that will be quite impossible. You see, Miss Tibbs is dead.'

Twenty Three

I SAT ON THE DUSTY GROUND of the plain, Mr. Quibble, my unwelcome companion standing over me at my side. As a child, when I heard about the Kaharian, from some of the tales Tibbs told us in our beds, everyone was transformed into beautiful creatures of flawless humanity. Alas, Innocent Quibble was still as fat, greasy and loathsome as he had been in the land of men.

He offered me a hand to help lift me from the floor.

'I can manage, thank you,' I said stubbornly as I picked myself off the dusty baked ground.

I looked around the landscape, seeing nothing for miles, and yet noted, 'We are being watched.' In truth, I cannot be sure that I actually said that, but in subsequent times I have discovered for a fact that we *were* being watched, and I am quite convinced I would have had the wit and wisdom to have sensed this.

We set out on our march in silence. Despite his short, pudgy legs, Quibble kept a brisk pace, and I sometimes found myself almost jogging alongside to keep up.

The heat was unrelenting, the purple sun, though not burning when you looked at it, emanated great warmth that made my skin prickly.

'We must reach the tree by nightfall,' Quibble blustered, short of breath.

'And when is nightfall? The sun doesn't seem to have moved at all.'

'There is no way of telling. When night falls, it will fall. It could happen in two minutes, it could be in ten hours. Here there are no seasons, no clocks. The sun does not set, it simply fades away before reappearing again.'

'And how much farther must we walk?'

'Impossible to say. There is no measure of distance here either, and things do, well... tend to move around a bit. You'll have noticed that the tree seems to sometimes get farther away, and then closer, then farther again.'

'Then how does anyone find their way around?'

'That is why we must reach the tree. From there, all should become clearer. Knowledge can be found at Allon Bakuth, the tree of weeping.'

We walked on, but a question weighed heavily in my mind.

'Mr. Quibble. You have never been to the Kaharian before?'

'That is right, Master Joshua.'

'Then how do you know quite so much about it?'

'Ah, my boy. That is a very long story.'

Twenty Four

'DEAD?'

'I regret so.'

'But how can that be? We left just days ago, and she was in perfect health.'

'Health and life, Lucy, are very fragile things that can be taken from us in the twinkling of an eye. I think it is fair to say that she died of a broken heart, wouldn't you say, Picardo?'

The servant looked uncomfortable at the question. He straightened his neck and mumbled, 'In a manner of speaking, my Lord.'

The old devil smirked at Lucy as the horrible truth became clear.

'And how did her heart come to be broken, exactly?'

'Oh, you naïve young fool! It could not have been avoided. You truly thought I would let that foul, withered hag live? Give you the chance to have somewhere to run? No...' The veins at his temples began to throb as his eyes glowed green, venom pouring from his mouth. My grandfather carried on speaking, spitting out his hate, but Lucy had stopped listening.

Poor Tibbs, a good woman, who had never harmed man nor beast. Who had taken in two mewling, puking children in their infancy, and had reared them with kindness and perfect love. Murdered. Her life cut down for no other reason, but that her kindness and love would offer too cosy an alternative to our grandfather's heinous schemes.

Lucy looked up with tears bristling in her eyes to see the wicked beast laughing. Laughing!

She turned her back on him and ran into the fire.

If Lucy thought that running back through the fire would bring her out into the sitting room that she had come in from, she learnt that she was mistaken within a few seconds.

The portal out of the Átjaró chamber instead took her straight into a dark, deep tunnel.

There was no light at all, but she kept on running, not really caring where it led, or what dangers there may be.

The tunnel led ever downwards, the smell was dank and moist. Lucy hoped the curving tunnel would lead her down to the sea. From there she could try to swim for the shore, or drown trying. She didn't care any more.

She had lost me. She had lost the woman who had cared for her for twelve years. There was nothing else that evil old daemon could take away from her except life itself.

Well, she wouldn't give him the pleasure.

The tunnel carried on turning, but something had changed. Lucy could feel the floor moving beneath her, shifting, twisting under her feet. She kept running, hoping her little legs would carry her. The noise of hydraulic pumps filled the labyrinth and she suddenly realised that the floor that was leading downwards was now suddenly heading up again. Lucy quickened her pace as panic beset her, when suddenly... *thump!*

She ran straight into a wooden door at full pace, and the black of the tunnel became darker still as her eyes closed and the blackness took her.

Twenty Five

THE SEARING HEAT HAD LOST ITS INTENSITY as we reached the shade of the outer branches of the vast tree that loomed over us.

As we had approached it, it became clear that the tree we had seen as we started our walk what seemed like a dozen hours ago was truly enormous. It stretched hundreds of feet into the air, and its branches seemed to cover an area the size of the entire village we'd lived in with dear Tibbs.

And yet on just one of those branches was there any sign of life. The rest of the fruitless arms were charred, as if by fire. But on one branch – a low hanging one (although not low-hanging enough for my twelve-year-old body to reach, even on tiptoes) hung a single piece of fruit. I can't tell you what type of fruit it was, since I had never seen one before, and I was never to taste this one (in case you were wondering!)

We made our way under the canopy of lifeless wood toward the giant trunk. Quibble set down the small bag and water bottle he carried on his shoulder and removed his overcoat. He gestured for me to sit down, propped against the trunk, and as I did, he placed his coat over me and offered me the water bottle.

I swigged and thanked him, and for the first time, I am sure I saw him smile.

I tried my luck at befriending this strange man. 'You are a kind man, really, aren't you?'

'I am a weak man, Joshua – a weak man. And my weakness has led to many unkind things being done by my hand.'

'I am sorry.'

'It is I who should be sorry, and yet I am not, which doesn't make me a very kind person at all. I sometimes think kind things, I sometimes even say kind things, and yet when it comes to the crunch, my actions are very far removed from those thoughts and words.'

I sat in silence, not really knowing how to react to the toad-man's willing, but unrepentant, confession.

He continued, 'This place is known as Allon Bakuth – the tree of weeping. In the desert plain, this single tree grows from the moisture of the tears of the souls that have fallen here, who were unable to resist the lure of temptation.

'You asked me earlier how I came to know so much about the Kaharian, although I have never before been here. Do you like books, Joshua?'

'I love them.'

'As did I when I was your age. I studied them fastidiously. I went to a school with other children in the town where my family lived. The other students picked on me because of my strange appearance.'

I looked away, not wanting to stare at his warty visage.

'Oh yes, I know people still recoil slightly when they see me. Even my own parents did. And yet I cannot show my own son the affection I wish I had received. What an unkind, selfish fool I am...'

He tailed off, lost in his own thoughts. It was some time before he spoke again.

'I loved books. My favourites were always the stories about the old times, when spirits walked among men and angels conversed with humans. My parents encouraged me. They took me to the temple each week and as I grew older, I began to learn that the stories I had studied were not stories at all – they were true!

'I became zealous in my reading and was soon regarded the brightest boy in the school. And I was proud! I was so proud of what I had achieved. The other boys still laughed and called me "fatty toad-face", but I was top of the class, and it was I who won the scholarship to study in the capital. It was I who had the last laugh!'

Passion blazed in Quibble's eyes momentarily, lost in happier times, before the sadness returned.

'So, I went off to the metropolis. There are all sorts of oddities in the city streets. There I could blend in. There the only thing anyone found remarkable about me was my knowledge of the Kaharian and its tales. Others came to me and asked me to tell them about the Pidaja and his Kaharian realm and how they could be more like me in his ways! People wanted to be like me! Can you imagine!

'One day, one such person came to me. He had heard of my great repute on all things scriptural and wanted to learn from me. He was an incredibly bright young chap. A couple of years younger than me. Handsome, charming, charismatic. He asked me to teach him all I knew, and in return he would teach me all his knowledge.'

'Who was he?'

'He called himself Lucian Strafe. It wasn't his real name, of course, but that would become known to the whole world in due course.

'And now, Master Joshua, you should rest.'

'But how can I rest when you have hardly told me anything of how you know about the Kaharian? I assume my grandfather...'

'Do not mention his name. Rest now, and I will tell you more in the morning. You remind me of my boy, you know. You have less fur, and not such sharp teeth, and you can speak in sentences when he can't, but other than that you're very much alike: always curious; always seeking knowledge.'

'That's good, isn't it? To want to know more?'

'Knowledge can be dangerous if you don't have the discernment to use it.'

As he spoke, he looked up to the single piece of fruit that hung suspended from the mighty tree that was our home for the night.

It was at this point that I fell asleep, I believe. I know that the next thing that happened was some hours later as I heard a scratching and scrambling that woke me from my slumber.

'Must eat! Feel so hungry! Need to eat more, feel more, know more!'

Through the branches above, a bright full moon shone, enough to light Innocent Quibble as he tried to scale the trunk of the tree, ever straining for the fruit that lay tantalisingly out of his reach.

'Just one more step. One more step for knowledge to be complete. To know as he knows. To see as he sees.'

The moon shone now on Quibble's round face, and his eyes blazed pure white in the moonlight, wide open and unblinking as he stretched out for the fruit that lay beyond him.

'Mr. Quibble. Get down! You will fall!'

'But I am so close! So close to the knowledge I have yearned for!'

As he spoke, he managed to grip one of his chubby hands onto the branch and then the other, and steadily he made his way along the branch toward the orb that he so desired, his eyes never swerving from that plump, juicy morsel.

As I stared at it, suddenly it seemed to take me too; though I felt no hunger, the longing was sudden and intense. *I must eat of the fruit!*

My eyes were gazing intently on my goal that Quibble now edged toward. I must get there before him! My heart was pumping, my eyes were wide. I felt like I had when Tibbs gave me my first cup of Moorish coffee – alert and alive!

I dug my fingernails into the bark of the ancient tree and started to climb as fast as I could toward the branch where Quibble now hung, scuttling sideways along it like a rhino-shaped crab.

I reached the branch in no time, and with great dexterity, swung onto it, facing forward and passing one hand in front of the other, like the monkeys I had seen in the zoo.

I was gaining ground on Quibble, nearer and nearer, though my eyes were firmly fixed on that beautiful fruit. As I reached the older man, I bashed against him, my legs kicking out as he came within striking distance of our prize.

'Let me past!' I yelled. 'I need to eat!'

Quibble may have replied, but I don't recall, for at that moment, as the two of us moved toward the end of the branch and within reach of our target, there was an almighty *thwack*. The spell was broken as I shook my head and turned back to see the branch was giving way at the trunk. It was too late, and all too suddenly the branch, along with its three occupants – Quibble, myself and fruit – came crashing to the earth with a bruising jolt.

We landed in tangled heap of limbs, the wind well and truly knocked out of us. The piece of fruit rolled down a small hill. Quibble quickly untangled himself from me, brushing me off and gave chase. The fruit came to rest only a few yards away and then just dissolved into nothing.

Quibble stood, stooping where he had been to pick up the imagined object of his desire. He shook his head as he came to.

'Oh my!' he exclaimed. 'What has become of me? Knowledge can be a dangerous thing, young man. A very dangerous thing.'

I never replied to his words. I remained seated where I had fallen, looking off into another direction.

My attention was now firmly fixed on a point around twenty feet away from me. Or rather, I should say, two points, as what I was looking at through the pre-dawn light was unmistakably a pair of bright green eyes.

Twenty Six

THE LIGHTS SEEMED TO SWIRL above her as Lucy awoke. Her head was thumping. She tried to lift her head from the pillow, but just couldn't.

'There now! Rest! Don't try to move, just lay back and close your eyes. The pain will pass.'

The voice was soothing, and as Lucy fell back into the pillow and closed her eyes, she made out the slight but strong frame of Picardo as he laid his hand softly on her forehead.

Lucy kept her eyes closed as Picardo gently massaged her temples with the tips of his fingers, coaxing her back to sleep.

Through the fog of her headache and tiredness she heard the servant speak again, but this time to another in the room.

'She must rest here, and is not to be moved. You have scared the child!'

'That is regrettable, of course...'

'It is more than regrettable...'

'Oh, come now, Picardo. The halo doesn't suit you. You and I are so deep in blood that sin will pluck on sin! Remember who you are. Remember what you are. Have you suddenly developed a conscience?'

Lucy heard the servant push back his chair violently as he stood:

'Yes, I have a conscience. It's time you did, too.'

'Oh, please! It is nearly the endgame, old friend! Soon, we will have the secret in our very hands and eternity will be ours! There is no need to pretend to be good!'

'Maybe I want to be good, to not pretend. I was good once... and so were you.'

'That was a long time ago; a very long time.'

Lucy heard Picardo sigh and leave the room. There was quiet until our grandfather came and sat in the chair beside the bed.

'A very long time ago.'

'What was a long time ago, Grandfather?' Lucia said, opening one eye.

The old devil looked down on her. 'What did you say?'

'What was a long time ago?'

'No, after that.'

'Grandfather.'

He looked at her hard for a long time, Lucia now opened her other eye, and tried to discern what he was thinking, but his leathery features gave no clue. His eyes, although penetrating, seemed somehow distant. Then, just as she was about to look away, from nowhere it came!

In the corner of one of the old man's large, black, soulless eyes it grew, small at first, but then brimming onto his lower eyelid, until this dam could hold it no longer and it broke into a rivulet, cascading down his wrinkled, hardened cheek. A single tear.

He quickly wiped it away with the back of his hand and recovered himself.

'I'm sorry, my child. It's just I've never been called Grandfather before.'

'What did you say?' Lucy said, still slightly dazed.

'I said, "I've never been called Grandfather before."'

'No, before that.'

'I said...' He paused now, his mouth dry as he tried to form the words. 'I said, "I'm sorry."'

Twenty Seven

I DON'T REMEMBER EXACTLY what I felt at the time, but my heart, that had beat so fast after our fall from the tree, seemed suddenly to stop.

My eyes fixed first on the two eyes, bright in the semi-darkness. The eyes were low, just inches from the ground, and as my senses adjusted, I started to make out the outline of the creature's lithe frame. The breaking light reflected on the sleek black fur, as it leaned forward, crouched and waiting. Ready.

My eyes didn't move as I spoke. 'Mr. Quibble?'

'Yes, boy, what is it? I was so very close to…'

I cut in, not wanting him to startle the animal.

'I want you to turn around very, very slowly and walk toward me.'

'I really can't imagine what all the fuss is ab…' His words dried as his eyes met those of the beast. 'Is that what I…?'

'I have only ever seen a drawing in a book, but I think it is a pantera.'

'Quite.'

'Known to kill a full-grown man with one lash of its claws.'

'Quite.'

The creature stretched out its claws, to illustrate the point, and pulled back his thin black lips into a snarl to expose long, white fangs, gleaming against the jet black of its fur.

'Any ideas what we are meant to do?'

'Up the tree again?' the fat fool panted, his breath still shallow from his earlier excursion.

'They can climb trees! I read about it. Let us just move very slowly away. Do not stop for your coat, just keep your eyes fixed on his eyes, and back away.

'And then?'

'And then hope he loses interest!'

We slowly edged our feet away from the beast, shuffling humbly, almost bowing in deference to its awesome power. I did not have a plan for getting out of there. We were in the middle of a seemingly unending desert, and the chances of us outrunning a pantera were slim. Certainly slimmer than Quibble's markedly un-streamlined waistline, that much is for certain!

As we kept on backing away, the creature inched its way toward us. We were keeping our distance, but not gaining ground. This game of cat and mouse could go on for hours, and there was only going to be one winner – and it wasn't going to be us mice (or toad!)

We kept feeling our way backwards with our feet, when all of a sudden, there was a new sensation. The parched, dusty firmament suddenly gave way to something softer, fresher. Grass!

I allowed myself to steal a glance behind me, and saw a wonder I could only have prayed for.

For there, in the middle of the arid plain, harboured under the vast canopy of the tree of weeping, was a small, quaint cottage, with a white wooden fence surrounding a neat garden.

Quibble had also noticed it, and we edged together toward the gate, opening it behind our backs and then bolting for the door. The door itself was not locked and we swung it open and crashed it shut, catching a flash of black, rippling muscle as the pantera bounded the fence and thrashed its razor-like claws against the sturdy timber door.

We stood breathless, leaning against that life-saving portal, listening to the snorts and snarls of the creature beyond, frustrated at losing his prey.

Minutes passed before either of us dared to speak.

'I didn't see this last night, did you?' I asked.

'No, I am sure...'

'That is because it wasn't here,' another voice cut in. 'I think you had better sit down.'

TWENTY EIGHT

WE TURNED AROUND TO SEE the orator of those words.

It was a small man. When I say small, I mean small. He stood no more than a foot and a half in his boots. His hair was frizzy and thin, his face lined, but the skin bright and rouged. He peered at us with small eyes through thick, rimless glasses.

'Well, do sit down, friends. I've been expecting you.'

He was dressed in an immaculate white shirt with a high collar and dark neck-tie. Over this was a tailored waistcoat with silk lapels. From the waistcoat pocket he drew on a chain, that I first expected to end in a watch, but as he pulled it from his pocket, a large bunch of keys emerged. He walked swiftly toward the door on his little legs, his whole body seeming to sway from side-to-side as he did. He reached high above him and inserted a key into the lock, turning it until it until the mechanism clicked.

'There! That should keep our feline friend out of harm's way!'

Quibble and I looked at each other, concerned that a locked door would be no obstacle to the creature.

'I am not sure that...' Quibble started.

'Oh, dear friend,' our tiny new acquaintance chipped in, 'in this neck of the woods, when I lock a door, then the door is locked, and none shall pass!'

Neither of us understood, but in this strange place where there was so little that we understood, it was becoming second nature to let these things go!

'Now, I have some tea brewing and some scones that are still warm from the oven. Master Joshua, would you prefer something cold to drink, as I know it is very warm outside? Some lemonade perhaps?'

'You know my name?'

'Oh yes! And Mr. Quibble here, too! It is my job to know the names of those who pass through here.'

Quibble was visibly perturbed that our 'secret' mission was perhaps not so secret after all. He said, 'I am Innocent Quibble, sir, but I am afraid you have the advantage over us, as we do not yet know your name.'

'Forgive me, dear chap! The excitement of visitors has made me quite forget myself. Hadraniel Derwood, at your service.'

'Delighted, I am sure,' continued the blustering solicitor. 'What is it you do here, Mr. Derwood?'

'I lock doors, and I unlock them!'

'It doesn't sound like a real job! Locking and unlocking doors? I am a solicitor.' My toad-like companion blustered showing anything but humility.

'And not a very good one, Mr. Quibble. You seem to forget that I know all about you. When was the last time you won a case?'

'Well, I...'

Silence hung in the air for a moment, before Derwood broke it: 'To put it in terms a legal man might enjoy, Mr. Quibble, judge not lest ye be judged!'

He chuckled away to himself, delighted at his quip. He wiggled over to the table, pulling himself up onto a normal-sized chair and then bounding up a pile of cushions so that he could see over the table. He gestured for us to join him.

'Yes, I lock and unlock doors. Not very skilled, one might say, unless you knew that every turn of the key carries an enchantment that holds a mighty power. For the key itself is but a lowly thing, but the one in whose name I turn it is the highest of the high. His name can access the deepest oceans and the tallest mountains. His name can halt the tide and make the seas part!

'I am but a little man, but bestowed in me is the greatest authority, for I am the second gatekeeper of the Kaharian!'

Quibble chuckled, 'Then I do not think much of your security, Mr. Derwood, for we have passed no *first* gatekeeper!'

'You fat fool! You trod the path of fire and water, and you think that gate is not kept! To tread that path, you walked the path of faith. That is the greatest guardian of all! Those who do not have the faith to walk through the fire and water do not have the faith to believe there is a kingdom beyond.'

Quibble was slighted by his apparent lack of understanding, and looked down at his feet, muttering inaudibly under his breath.

'Excuse me, Mr. Derwood,' I said attempting to regain some harmony in the conversation, 'what is it that lies beyond the second gate?'

'Aha! An intelligent question! Finish your tea, young man, and I will show you!'

I would love to tell you I swallowed down the hot brew in one gulp, in eager anticipation of where our journey would next lead us. However, the journey so far had left me in little doubt that the road ahead would not be easy. With that thought in mind, I smiled politely at the little man, and took small sips from the steaming cup.

Twenty Nine

IT WAS NOT A WORD THAT CAME EASILY from our grandfather's lips. In fact, it may never have passed them before, at least never when he had meant it with any sincerity.

However, no sooner had the words penetrated the air than he pushed back hard in his chair, sending it tumbling, and vanished from the room.

On the counterpane close to Lucy's right hand, a small circular spot of damp, the mark of his fallen tear, was all the evidence there was of an old daemon's humanity.

There was a gentle knock at the door, and Lucy pushed herself up a little in the bed.

'Come in!' she chimed, although the words clattered in her still aching head.

Picardo's long fingers pushed around the door and he poked his head into view to see the patient. He smiled at Lucy and walked his gangly walk to her bedside, where he sat next to her.

He looked down at her and smiled again. His face was kind but melancholy, as though he had known a lifetime of sadness.

If she only knew of that sadness.

Antonius Picardo had been a young soldier, an ace oarsman, runner, marksman, with but one weakness: a kind and loving heart.

He was given rank at a young age and fought in many campaigns, all of them victorious. He didn't have much taste for enemy blood, but he was a keen strategist, and a fearsome athlete. The simple sight of him lined up in opposition sent many a foe running before the first shot had been fired. Yet fighting never fulfilled him as much as the love of Amara.

Amara was one of the Nephilim, and was as beautiful as any of the angels of heaven.

He had first met her when he was on leave in a coastal town from one of his victorious campaigns. For a warrior like him, women were freely available at every turn. In the tavern at night, on the streets, in the amphitheatre where he was accorded a hero's welcome. But not one of those women tempted him, though they were beautiful in their scarlet robes, with sun-kissed skin and dark, exotic eyes.

He saw her as he paused for rest on his morning run. Her morning chores brought her into the centre of the town from her parents' farmstead to draw water from the well. Her dress was simple, plain even, her feet bare, her hair silken, the fairest strawberry blonde, hanging loose. And her face! That face! Unlike the olive-skinned local girls, this was a face of the finest porcelain, unblemished, delicate features with bright green eyes shining under long eyelashes.

As he saw her, he stepped back into the early morning shadows, not wanting to be seen. He just stood peering from the cover of a nearby wall watching her every graceful move.

Having filled the bucket, she started to move off from the well and the young Picardo followed her at a safe distance, not wanting her to be alerted or alarmed by his presence. She headed out of the town on the country road and across a field, up the hill toward a far-off farm.

As she tried to straddle and climb the gate without spilling the water, she stumbled slightly on the dry stone wall. She hit the ground first, followed by a torrent of water, and then a heavy wooden bucket.

Instinctively, the young general broke cover to help her, and as he hurdled the wall, he found this angel of a girl lying flat on her back, drenched through and laughing the most musical laugh he had ever heard. Her ethereal beauty enchanted him.

That was the first of many meetings that summer. Endless hours were spent lying in the tall grass looking at the sky together, talking or sometimes just silently taking in the moment, listening to the other breathe. The warrior had spent so long in mindless, blood-soaked battles, dreaming that one day he would see true beauty. And now he did not merely want to see beauty, he wanted to be a part of it.

He and his beloved Amara became inseparable. Until, of course, they were inevitably and tragically separated.

THIRTY

HADRANIEL DERWOOD WAS A QUIRKY little fellow. His frizzy hair was neatly parted in the centre, his rimless glasses sat on the low bridge of his short, slightly curved nose, and just below was a thin, wispy moustache that curled slightly at the ends.

He moved with some haste now along what seemed to be a very long corridor in his small cottage. Although he moved hurriedly, Quibble and I were able to keep pace at an ambling stroll owing to our legs being much longer than those of the curious little man.

The corridor was featureless, panels of wood on either side, but with no doors or recesses or anything to identify one part of the corridor from another. However, as we walked, it felt as though the corridor was getting smaller, the ceiling lower somehow. At least that's how it seemed, as Mr. Derwood, who was now a little way ahead of us, did not appear quite so small any more, so either the corridor was shrinking or...

...he was growing!

As this new reality dawned on me, we came to a dead stop. Mr. Derwood turned and faced us, now towering over us. His light voice had become deeper, and resonated along the walkway as he addressed the cowering solicitor and me.

'Foolish you have been to believe what your eyes have shown you. Even he who sent you warned you not to believe the evidence of your eyes.'

Quibble's voice trembled as he spoke. 'You know who sent us?'

Mr. Derwood was icy calm as sweat began to bead on my brow: 'Oh yes. Though I will not speak his name, I am well aware of the schemes of our exiled "friend".'

The way he spoke the word 'friend' chilled me. We were discovered. Our mission thwarted at the first hurdle. We would surely die, and I would never see Lucy again.

'I have told you that a mighty power is invested in me as a gatekeeper. Egress is granted only to those I admit by a simple test. Only those who pass the test will be given the pass key.'

'And those who fail?' I asked, not really wanting to know the answer.

He slowly, deliberately looked me and my colleague in the eye before answering: '*Pffffft!* Your existence will be eradicated, blotted from the book of life. There will be simply... nothing!'

I swallowed hard. I had faced more life and death situations in the past day than in the previous twelve years of my once happy life. Was there some grace that would see me survive again now?

'I want you to close your eyes now,' the enlarged Mr. Derwood said softly, almost songfully. I breathed deeply as I stood in silence awaiting the next instruction. I heard Quibble do the same, though his breaths were shorter, as though holding back tears. 'You need not speak a word, as I will hear the voice of your souls in the silence. I have one simple question, and only the first thought that comes forth from your heart will be accepted as your answer. For whom do you want to succeed in your mission?'

The air went still. Thoughts flashed into my head. Which had I thought first? What was the 'right' answer that Mr. Derwood was looking for? I kept my eyes tightly shut, trying to concentrate on one thought. Nothing seemed to happen for several seconds, and then gently I felt something cold pressing from the inside of my tightly clenched fist. I slowly dared to open my eyes and looked down at my hand. The knuckles, white from anxiety, gripped tightly, but I lightly unfurled my stiff fingers to reveal the new contents of my palm.

A key.

Thirty One

PICARDO SAT ON AN AGED WOODEN CHAIR at the bedside and smiled down on Lucy.

His eyes had a distant expression. Lucy, though still dazed from her accident, looked deeply into the old man's face. My sister was quite wise beyond her years and could often see beyond a person's outer countenance.

'Mr. Picardo, you seem so very sad when you are alone.'

The elderly servant checked himself and straightened up at the suggestion, then his shoulders relaxed as he spoke, 'You are a perceptive young lady, miss. I can see it would be pointless to lie to you.

'I know you do, and will, miss your brother very greatly for the time he is away. I too know what it is to grieve for someone very dear.'

'Someone you loved?'

'Yes, someone I loved deeply, and whom I miss to this day. She was the most wonderful person I ever knew.'

'What was her name?'

'Amara.'

Lucy began to sit up in her bed, the story beginning to interest even her concussed brain, 'It is a beautiful name. What happened to her?'

Picardo's eyes went dull and he stared vacantly across the room and out of the window where darkness had begun to settle in for the night.

'I killed her.'

Thirty Two

A KEY!

I couldn't believe what I saw. My gaze moved upwards. Mr. Derwood was nowhere to be seen. Then I looked down to my left hand side and there kneeling on the floor, silently shaking with tears, was Innocent Quibble.

He clutched an iron key like mine in his left hand.

'The Pidaja be praised!' he spluttered between now uncontrollable sobs.

I helped him to his feet. His fat hands that looked so oily were soft to touch, and he gripped firmly on my arm for support.

'We passed the test. We passed!' I said to him.

'So it would seem!' he replied. 'But we must be on our guard! Our presence and our purpose in the Kaharian is seemingly heralded. There will be trials at every corner from now on.'

We walked forward a few steps to a large wooden door with iron spikes studding it at regular intervals, and on the left hand side were two keyholes, one for each key.

'Two keyholes,' I said, pointing out the obvious, 'so we must walk through here together and return together.'

'Indeed, young man, and may I say, whatever may occur, I am grateful to have you as my travelling companion, Master Joshua.'

I didn't reply; I just looked into his sad eyes, and squeezed his pudgy hand in affirmation.

We inserted our keys into the locks and together we turned them. A complex internal mechanism seemed to whirr into action, and the solicitor asked, 'By the way, Master Joshua, what was your answer to the question? For whom do you wish to succeed and return with the box?'

'So many thoughts went through my head, but I believe my answer was my sister. I want to return so I can see her again. But something I don't understand, if you'll forgive me, is how you passed the test when you are here to do my grandfather's evil bidding?'

'I do not give a hoot about your grandfather's scheme! I am here for the sake of my son!'

THIRTY THREE

WITH QUIBBLE'S SURPRISING REVELATION reverberating in my head, we pushed the door open. What lay beyond was as surprising as my companion's last words: a small covered terrace with a table and two chairs under the canopy, and on the table an ice bucket with bottles of lemonade and a small selection of rolls and cakes. Mr. Derwood obviously wanted us to start the next stage of the journey on a full stomach!

I tucked in with my childish enthusiasm for all things sugary, and Quibble (his portly frame suggesting he also succumbed to sweet temptation on an all too regular basis) also popped a number of tasty treats into his wide mouth.

Our delight was enhanced by the fact that our food supply seemed to be self-replenishing. That is to say that as much as we ate, the pile never seemed to go down. Perhaps we could stay here forever or at least for a very long time.

The landscape beyond the terrace was very different from the one we had encountered on the other side of the cottage. Ahead of us was a verdant green landscape of lush grass, and in the sky above there were rain clouds for as far as the eye could see. The temperature was warm, but the rain beat down steadily on the canopy over our table.

As we sat back in comfort, our tummies full, I ventured to find out more about the man I travelled with.

'Mr. Quibble. When we were under the tree last evening you started to tell me about a man you met at university.'

'Ah, yes...' He was silent for a moment, just staring out at the rain-lashed landscape ahead. 'Are you sure you wish to know the man with whom you travel, whatever his story may entail?'

'Yes, I am sure. By now, I think very little could surprise me!'

'Oh my dear boy. You do not know the half of it! I am a villain,' he closed his eyes tightly, at the pain of these words, 'and villainous deeds have been done by these hands.'

'Tell me about that man. Was it Lucian…?'

'Lucian Strafe. You know the meaning of Lucian, of course, from your sister's name, but oh, what light he brought into my lonely, dark life of isolation and nothing but books, books and more books. What light!

'Lucian had a mind sharper than any I had known; still to this day, I have never met such an intellect. And so perceptive, so sensitive to the feelings of others, as though he could look into your soul and draw out the very thing that sorrowed you.

'He came to me to grow his knowledge of the tales of the Kaharian, and he offered to teach me what he knew of worldly things and to help me grow in confidence to find the thing I yearned for most.'

'And what was that?' I interrupted.

'A wife: I so wanted a wife who would love me for who and what I was. I was not blessed with looks or the swagger of youth. Never had I even dared start a conversation with a girl, and they only ever spoke to me to tell me to get out of the way.

'Lucian and I met regularly in a small tea house, and our meetings quickly became the highlight of my week. I would tell him the legends of the Kaharian and their meanings, he would question me with the smartest questions you could imagine, often making me question the very truth of the fabric of the argument I had spent years arriving at.

'He in turn was true to his word. One week he suggested we abandoned our usual meeting place to meet later in the evening in the bustling streets of the metropolis. I met him at our agreed rendezvous and without speaking he signalled for me to follow him into a dark alleyway. In the darkness of the passageway he turned to me and laid his hand atop my head. I closed my eyes, not quite knowing how to react, and I felt a rigour all through my muscles, a trembling all over my body. It lasted but a few seconds and as I opened my eyes, I saw Lucian smiling brightly at me.

'He took me by the hand, and led me into a lighter part of the alley where there was a shop window. There I caught my reflection, and saw not the dwarfish toad shape that I had come to despise over the years, but a normal young man – no, a *handsome* young man – transformed beyond all recognition!

'We went into one of the many dance halls where men, friends of Lucian, shook my hand, and women smiled at me. *Smiled at me!* It was then that I saw her. That kind face with the warmest of smiles, pretty and athletic in build, light brown hair neatly tied back. With unaccustomed confidence I went to her, and spoke. I was instantly charmed. The rise and fall of her foreign accent, and the openness and expressiveness of her love for the tales of the Kaharian meant we spent many long days together reading and visiting the temple.

'Lucian's enchantment was lasting. On my wedding day, I looked quite the handsome groom. My studies finished, I started to speak publically at the temple. People flocked to hear me and the new light I would cast on stories they could never fathom before.

'But as my popularity on the platform grew and grew, my own disenchantment with my own teaching escalated.

'My meetings with Lucian had continued and he was a regular dinner guest at our house. I was forever in his debt. That house where we dined was built on the profits of his life-changing transformation. But as we spoke of the things of the Kaharian, he would drop questions in, questions I could never answer, but always left me doubting my own beliefs.

'It started to show in my teaching, too. I had, to that point, held the audiences with my encyclopaedic knowledge and total command of my subject, and now there were doubts, questions that crept into my talks and sent my listeners away not enlightened but confused.

'I came home one day and sat alone in my study and I noticed a slight yellowing of my skin and two small but very distinct warts starting to grow at the base of my thumb.

'My wife was calling me for dinner, but I ignored her as I fled for the door and along the busy city streets to the gate I had seen

Lucian enter his house by many times without ever crossing the threshold myself.

'He immediately saw how shaken I was and invited me in. His house was the strangest place I had seen; only shards of illumination coming from narrow leaded windows, throwing light on walls of dark velvet drapes, burgundies, purples, and where the light came in, the air seemed thick with incense and a strange, horrible smell, like burnt flesh.

'He led me along the corridor and opened a heavy door to a large, square room, and what I saw is still etched in my mind.

'On the dusty floorboards was a crudely chalk-drawn shape: a star with five points. At the head of the star, straight ahead of me, was a magnificent, intricately carved wooden throne which sat empty, and from which I assumed Lucian had risen to come to my aid. Then my attention was drawn to the other points of the star; at the apex of each was a simple wooden chair.

'It was not the chairs themselves that startled me though. Rather their occupants.

'They were angels.'

'Angels?' was the best, the *only*, response I could come out with. 'On the earth?'

'And that was my thought, too, young man. My mind swam. Although I believed in angels from my study and faith in scripture, I never ventured to believe that I would meet one; and here, at the home of Lucian Strafe, who had done so much to question my beliefs, to cast doubt on the truth of the scripture I held dear, here he was, in conference with the sentinels of the Kaharian.'

'Did they speak to you?'

'"Do not be afraid!" said one of them. They have a habit of greeting humans like that. I suspect as most humans who meet angels tend to be very afraid!

'They were magnificent. Even though seated, they were tall, with grace and poise, immaculately robed in white, their faces beautiful, elegant, delicate but cold with eyes of ice blue and strong cheekbones.'

'And wings?'

'And wings, of course! But as my thoughts began to slow to a normal speed and I started to process the scene, I could sense that something was very clearly wrong. The whole atmosphere of the place in which they were meeting was in complete contrast to their ethereal beauty. It was as dark as they were light.

'They sat in their respective chairs, unmoved, staring directly at me. Lucian too looked deep into my eyes and smiled. "You are welcome here, my friend. You are an able man, Innocent, and you may be of use to us. And if you are able to assist us, we would, naturally, be most happy to help you to overcome that which ails you."

'With that, Lucian turned his back on me, and to my surprise, slowly started to remove the long black cloak which he wore. As he did so, he seemed to grow in stature! Taller he grew! His thick, dark hair turned to white blond, and then from his back, which now faced me, started to emerge protrusions, growing, growing into beautiful wings, though not white as the other angels', but golden. He glided a few metres across the floor and perched, regally, on the throne at the head of the star.

'I was speechless. For what seemed like minutes, nothing was said. All I could do was fall to my knees before his great power.

'He chuckled: "Good! Your kneeling before my throne is a splendid start to our business, my dear friend! I am so pleased that I am at last able to share my little secret with you! Behold this assembly! Gathered to save the world of men from a malevolent power that would destroy it!"

'I looked up to the great one before me. "What is this power you speak of, my Lord, and how can I help in such a quest?"

'Lucian stood, rising high above my prostrate body. He exchanged looks and finally a smile with the other angels in the room. "You can help by becoming our loyal envoy. The malevolent power, who must be destroyed, is the Lord of Creation! We must destroy the Pidaja!"'

I interrupted, 'The Pidaja? But the Pidaja would never destroy his own people?'

'Of course he wouldn't, Joshua, but I was deeply in awe of Lucian's mighty power, and I believed every word he said, and I did take a vow of loyalty to him and this group of angels.

'He told me that he was in fact the Morning Star, one of the brightest angels of the skies. He had become disenchanted at the Pidaja's neglect for his human children and sought to negotiate a better deal for humankind by positive dialogue, or by force if necessary.

'He also introduced me to the four other angels, who were four watchers, sentinels protecting the four corners of the Kaharian. I was instantly drawn to the watchman of the North, who kept his base in the fiefdom of Kerioth.'

'My grandfather!'

'Indeed, it was he, although let us not mention his name further, lest we be overheard.

'He was the most striking of all the angels; a warrior, a strategist. I became his loyal subject, and he the most loyal master.

'He healed me of my disfigurement. I just couldn't bear the thought of my dear wife knowing the truth about the beast she had married. She is the finest woman I have known: kind beyond understanding at times.

'For my part, I became your grandfather's follower.'

'What did you do for him?'

'It was very simple, really. He asked me to keep teaching in the temple, but he asked me to challenge my listeners, question if they really believed the Pidaja was good and just in their lives. And then... and then, and I am skipping ahead here, Joshua, but when the time of the great battle came, he asked me for a list of names of those who attended the temple and were loyal to the Pidaja.'

'What happened to them?'

'Not one of them saw another spring.'

No tear welled in his eye, in fact his tone was abrupt, matter-of-fact. Did he not care about the loss of people he knew, who had followed him and relied on him to lead them? Or was the hurt simply too much for him to bear?

He stood now. Clearly, his storytelling had ended, although so much remained unsaid.

'I think the rain is easing, Master Joshua.' It was an optimistic forecast as sheets of the wet stuff pelted the canopy over our heads, but we had to move sometime, and it seemed that time was now.

'Will it be safe out there, in the long grass? There doesn't even seem to be a path,' I proffered, hoping there might be time for another cake, or perhaps even just to stay right there forever.

'We will follow a straight course. Wherever we head is where we are meant to be headed.'

I didn't even question his strangely riddled answer.

'As for whether it will be safe, Master Joshua: I very much doubt it!'

THIRTY FOUR

'YOU KILLED HER?' MY SISTER TREMBLED as she spoke the words. The kindly servant seemed so gentle and yet there was a dark heart to his story, it seemed. 'But you said you loved her!'

'And I did,' Picardo continued to stare out of the window, 'but I had a greater love.'

'Another lady?'

'Oh no, Miss Lucy; my love, or my lust, was for power. Terrible, awesome power!

'When I was a young man, I was a soldier; a general, in fact. I had no desire for bloodshed, but I had a great strategic mind, and I loved to keep my people, my country safe from the hordes who would pillage our land.

'I met Amara when I was on leave. And I loved her instantly, and she loved me.

'However, on my return to the front, I met a man, or what I believed to be a man, who would change my life. That man was your grandfather.'

Picardo stood now and made his way over to the window, looking out through the lead-latticed panes at the lake. The dim moonlight caught him as he turned his face back to the bed and continued to address Lucy. 'Lord Aquila was dressed as any man would dress, and he charmed me instantly with the most devastating form of persuasion – he made me feel indispensable, he made me feel unbeatable.

'He told me that he had heard tell of my great victories on the battlefield, and how highly regarded I was by my comrades, and how feared I was by my enemies.

'He told me that the time was coming when a great battle would be fought, that there were mysterious forces at work behind the scenes seeking to bring the forces of chaos on the world of men.

'I did not fully understand his cryptic speech, but he left me with a decidedly uncryptic ultimatum. He told me this would be the battle for the future of mankind, and I must decide whose side I was on. Then he left.

'There was no question of whose side I was on. In that brief conference, I had come face-to-face with the most charismatic, powerful person I had ever met. I had fought alongside field marshals, I had given counsel on battles to kings and princes of men. Not one of them could hold me in their power like this simple, charming man in a finely tailored suit. There were no airs or graces, just sheer, awesome… majesty!'

Lucy sat stunned at the passion now flowing through the old man as he recalled his lost youth.

'My mind raced for days, knowing I must find the man and pledge my allegiance to him. I didn't sleep. Eventually I was free from my duties to go into the village near where our battalion was stationed. He had left me no instruction other than that when I looked for him, I would find him.

'True to his word, and I knew not how, as soon as I entered the tavern, there he was.

'On that night, I vowed to serve him to the ends of the earth and beyond, for as long as I had life in my body. In return, he promised me a seat at the right hand of the Throne of Glory, where I would be exalted and hailed by people of all nations.

'Although your grandfather is a fearsome man, Miss Lucy, do not mistake me in this. I was not enslaved to him out of fear, but by my own hunger for acclaim and power.

'He told me, we must leave at once to consult with his council of war. I asked him one thing: to allow me to say farewell to my beloved Amara.

'He himself took me in his carriage to the farm where she lived with her family, or at least with her mother. Like your own father, she was one of the Nephilim – her father was an angel of the Kaharian.

'I said a short but loving goodbye to my dear girl. It was not out of the ordinary. A soldier's lot is full of goodbyes, hoping, praying you will return home to see the ones you love again.

'As I closed the door behind me and approached Lord Aquila's carriage, I saw he was holding out a sword to me.

'I took it to be a gift to bring success in battle, but as I grasped its handle in my hand, the metal burned hard, and yet I did not let go, could not let go.

'He looked stonily at me, his lip curled and he spoke just two words: "Kill her!"

'I tried to reason with him, I argued for what seemed like hours to let her live, but he was remorseless. For him, any human emotion would make me weak in battle. As long as I had something to return home to, I would not be able to freely offer my life to the great cause he said he fought for. He said that it was easier this way, as the enemy would come for Amara when I was gone and she would die a torturous and agonising death at their hands.'

Tears welled in the sunken eyes of the elderly manservant and trickled down his gaunt cheeks.

'Finally, as I continued to refuse, Lord Aquila took a dagger from his belt, and started toward the door of the farmhouse. I ran after him, trying to stop him, but he was strong. As we reached the door I managed to halt his progress, and breathlessly said, "If it must be done, I will do it." He showed no emotion, he just unlatched the door and ushered me inside as he started to walk away to the carriage.

'I made my way silently up the stairs, the sword of fire still tight in my grasp. I knelt by my dear one's bed, taking in her breathtaking beauty one last time. I gently kissed her on the forehead and stood with my sword high above me.'

Both the storyteller and the listener were now in tears. There was no more to be said. Picardo collapsed to his knees where he had stood, and my sister – my dear, sweet, compassionate sister –

climbed from her bed, walked over to him, and held him in her arms.

Thirty Five

THE LONG GRASS WAS THICK and dense. Innocent Quibble carried with him a collapsible walking cane, and I was grateful that he did, as it made our progress through the undergrowth swifter as he hacked a way ahead.

We were but a short distance into our journey, but already our clothes were drenched with sweat. I didn't mind in the slightest. Many a time Lucy and I had spent a whole summer's day running around, before jumping feet first into the farmer's pond. Mr. Quibble, though, looked most out of sorts.

His coat, he had thankfully given up when we were confronted by the pantera, and now he removed his jacket and neck tie and undid the buttons of his waistcoat. He also shed the white gloves that he permanently seemed to don, revealing pudgy, warty hands, the fingers slightly webbed in appearance.

Poor Mr. Quibble was not cut out for long distance trekking. However, despite his obvious fatigue, and that his cotton shirt was now transparent against his skin, he kept thrashing a path onwards, though we knew not where.

This continued for some time before we stopped and opened a bottle of lemonade we had taken with us from our patio buffet.

The once icy drink was now the same temperature as the warm air around us, and the liquid exploded from the bottle as I removed the cap. There was still plenty left and we both swigged gratefully of the fizzy warm liquid.

There we both sat for a moment, dizzy with exhaustion, longing for some fresh air to breathe rather than the humid fug around us.

There were no insects, no flies, but the air seemed somehow thicker, as though swimming through syrup.

In my tiredness, I asked that most childish of questions: 'Do you think we are nearly there yet?'

Quibble, still panting and gulping the last of the lemonade, spluttered, 'There is no way of knowing when we do not know where we are headed, or even if we are going in the right direction.'

I sighed deeply, and looked back at the wide path we had hacked through the vegetation.

I chuckled to myself and without thinking said something that I knew as soon as I opened my mouth would come back to bite me: 'We may not know where we are headed, but if anyone were following us, they would have a very good idea of the way we came.'

Quibble looked apprehensively at me, and I at him, and we both stood together, silently collecting our few things.

'Maybe I will put my stick away now, Joshua. It may take longer, but for caution's sake, let us not leave a track.'

So we continued on our now more discreet path.

Thirty Six

PICARDO WIPED THE TEARS from his eyes with the tips of his fingers closed together.

He looked up at my sister, whose own tears welled. 'How can you hold a cold-blooded murderer in your arms? How can you even bear to look at me after what I have just told you?'

And my sister, being the person she was, didn't say a word; she just continued to hold him.

MORNING DAWNED OVER KERIOTH.

My sister was now returned to her bed. Picardo, eyes red from crying, was asleep in a sturdy armchair in the corner; his mouth open, gently snoring.

Lucy soundlessly arose. As she caught her reflection in the mirror on the dressing table, she caught sight of the small bandage on her forehead. With everything else that had happened, she had quite forgotten her collision with a door.

It had been a night of tears. Her own, Picardo's terrible confession, and a single rivulet from the normally unyielding eyes of our grandfather.

She pulled back the heavy, dusty curtains, throwing daylight on the room.

Picardo stirred with a snort, initially perplexed as to where he was. He immediately pushed himself up from his resting place and looked panicked as he realised day had broken. He muttered, 'I must go,' and then did just that, leaving Lucy alone.

She rested now at the dressing table, heavily breathing in as she looked at the girl in the mirror. Her pretty eyes and nose were swollen from the tears of the night before, her lips reddened from biting on them as was her nervous habit.

For the first time in her life, she had awoken and I wasn't there, and although I have never been able to ask her for her thoughts at this moment, I sense she thought on me now, and Tibbs.

All Lucy knew in this moment was that Tibbs was dead. And yet I can reveal to you that our dear old guardian's part in this tale was not yet at an end. My grandfather had, surprisingly perhaps, told the truth when he informed Lucy that Tibbs had died, and from that I am sure you inferred that he had had the bright old lady disposed of, as indeed was the case. However, sometimes in the schemes of evil men, their ugly deeds have unexpected ends.

Lucy lingered at the dressing table for a little while, eventually picking up a hairbrush and pulling it through her knotted blonde waves.

While she hated the situation she found herself in, and despaired at the loss of her brother and her guardian in quick succession, she would face the situation with grace.

She shared a house with a daemon and a murderer, and yet she could bring something to that household that had been in short supply for too long.

Love.

Thirty Seven

I DON'T KNOW HOW LONG they had followed us, but as we tried to push our way carefully through the thick grasses and bushes that inhabited this lush green land, the sense grew that there was indeed something near.

At this point, whatever it was, or whoever it was, stayed well out of sight. In fact, there wasn't even a rustling sound or a movement, but just a growing feeling of apprehension at what might be out there.

Where we had previously been drenched with sweat, the rain now came again, ensuring every fibre we stood in was soaked through.

As the rain fell, the ground became heavy with mud, slowing our progress. If indeed we *were* making progress, as we still didn't actually know where we were going.

Part of our problem was that we both had rather short legs, mine on account of my tender years, and Quibble was just somewhat wider than he was tall.

Even if we had been more nimble on our feet, it is unlikely that we would have been able to outrun our pursuers.

Although we spoke not a word, I could tell Quibble could also sense something bearing down on us as he tried to move his squat legs more quickly through the cloying mud.

The soundless undergrowth started to bustle now with movement from all corners, and then it stopped. Quibble and I also ceased moving; waiting, listening, and then after a few breathless seconds, a voice.

'Lay down all that you are carrying and fall to your knees.' The voice was light but full of authority, and we were immediately at its mercy.

There was still no sign of man nor beast, but to our knees we fell and waited.

Gradually, shapes began to emerge through the thick forestation. Tall men, roughly dressed in greys and browns. They had the fashion style of herdsmen, but their soft faces and elegant hands suggested maybe some other calling.

One of the men stepped forward. Tall and powerfully built, he oozed authority. His fair beard was neatly trimmed and his long hair was tied back. His face was tanned, and there were fine wrinkles around his small but intense dark eyes.

He didn't speak a word as he approached us but his broad frame loomed over our cowering bodies.

As he got close to me, he swooped down and I suddenly felt myself lifted from the floor in his arms. He held me like a baby. I heard Quibble cry out in protest, but I heard not what he said as the man momentarily fixed me with his stare. From nowhere, another man appeared bringing with him a small pony, and in a second the leader firmly but carefully dispatched me from his arms onto the back of the animal.

Quibble, by this time, was on his feet, and protectively moved toward me, but the leader stepped into his path stopping him in his tracks by his sheer presence. And then he spoke... and that voice, oh, that voice of voices.

'Do not be afraid. We come in peace, travellers, and ask that you would be our guests.'

With an awestruck dipping of the head Quibble gave his assent; the troop fell swiftly, silently into formation, and we were on our way.

Thirty Eight

HER COURAGE RESTORED, Lucy made her way down the magnificent central staircase that dominated the main hall of Kerioth.

In her becalmed state, she started to absorb the detail of the carvings in the thick marble hand rail she clung to. As she studied the craftsmanship, she sharply withdrew her hand from the fine detailing of entwined serpents; twisting, turning toward the bottom of the rail, finishing with a triple-headed viper, its forked tongues extended and decorated in gold.

She shivered slightly at the sight. What was this place that her grandfather had made his home?

Her mind drifted to her first encounter with the castle and the sight of the thousands of eyes that watched her, Joshua and Picardo as they made their approach.

Lost souls.

Was she to join their number? Was a numb, pointless existence as a captive in this darkly beautiful prison, followed by a tortured afterlife in purgatory, all that awaited her now?

The question did not have long to dwell in her thoughts as her reverie was broken by a door opening below.

Our grandfather stood at the threshold and beheld Lucia looking down at him.

'My dear!' he croaked, his demeanour tired and his voice hoarse. 'It gladdens my heart to see you feeling better. I thought we might take tea in the library this morning? If that would please you?'

Lucy looked at the old monster, who seemed so frail from her lofty vantage point, before breathing deeply and smiling gently, 'Yes, that would be very nice.'

In these 'enlightened' times there are many great libraries in the world. Growing up, Lucy and I had considered our shared rickety pine shelf with a couple of dozen archaic children's books with faded technicolour illustrations, an atlas of the known world, and a book of scripture as our 'library'. In the sitting room, in amongst her collection of thimbles, Tibbs would keep linen-bound volumes with yellowed pages that smelt slightly of worn socks in a higgledy-piggledy fashion.

Neither of these experiences prepared Lucy for the sight she was about to encounter.

As she entered the room, following our grandfather, it was virtually dark. There was a musty, dank smell in the room and there was a sense that nobody had been in here for years.

Lord Aquila made his way cautiously along to the far end of the room mainly by feeling his way along pieces of (unseen) furniture.

'Let us have ourselves a little light, shall we?' he asked as he yanked at some heavy curtains at the far end.

Immediately the room was flooded with bright sunlight. Lucy shielded her eyes from the glare a little, and Aquila spluttered as the dusty curtains threw up a heavy plume of particles into the light.

As Lucy adjusted her eyes, she gasped at the sight that surrounded her.

'Oh my!' was all she could muster as she took in the seemingly endless line after line of immaculate leather tomes that adorned every wall. As her gaze lifted, she saw that the collection extended high into the air, maybe a hundred feet or more. At intervals there were small balconies and delicate spiral staircases adorned with silver and blue jewels, giving the impression of a waterfall.

Our grandfather struck a match and lit an oil lamp and as he did, another caught light, then another, then another; throughout the floor level and the five balconies above, light cascaded from floor to ceiling, and then finally in the chain reaction, a beautiful chandelier was aglow with hundreds of orbs illuminating the glittering crystal beads that were strung between them.

Primo Aquila let his gaze rest on the wonder in my sister's face. He brought his hands together in joy, and slowly lifted the tips of his fingers to his lips as he contemplated the radiance he saw.

'I hope so much that you will like it. It was... it was your father's favourite room.'

'My father?'

'Yes, Ahava was an avid reader. Very bright indeed. Much of the collection, I must confess, belonged to him and I hope...' he hesitated, checking his emotions, 'I hope you will consider yours now.'

'My father was called Ahava?'

'Why yes, of course!'

'I don't think I've ever heard his name before. He has always just been "Father" in my thoughts. It is a beautiful name.'

'And a fitting one. You are very much like him, I think.'

'I wouldn't know. Josh sometimes says he thinks he can remember our parents, but I think sometimes the mind creates that which it longs for.'

Silence hung in the air as both reflected on what that simple truth meant to them both. Lucy continued, 'What was my mother's name?'

'Your mother? Well, she was called Raya, and Joshua is her very likeness in spirit. Impetuous and headstrong... but full of faith, friendship and loyalty.'

'I'd like you to tell me about them.'

'I fear that would only cause you more pain, my dear.' Lord Aquila turned his back and looked out through the vast window toward the lake that glistened in the morning sun beyond.

'In any case, I would still like to know.'

He turned back to see Lucy's unwavering expression, averting his eyes toward the bookshelves momentarily, before looking again to see her gaze was unbroken.

'Very well,' he said, shrugging his shoulders. He moved to a bookcase close by, unlocked the glass door and laid his spidery hand on a slim volume within.

'Take a seat, child. I will have Picardo bring us some hot tea.'

THE SERVANT HAD BROUGHT in the tea without making eye contact with Lucy. His shame was writ large in his ashen face, though.

Lucy wanted to hold out a hand and just touch his arm in reassurance but she became distracted by the small book that had been laid on the table in front of her.

In contrast to the magnificent leather volumes that bedecked the walls everywhere she could see, this was rather a modest, flimsy thing; its paper cover was battered and dog-eared in its corners, and on the front was a handwritten title, "Night Song", but it was the words scribbled in a neat but childish hand in the bottom right corner that captivated her: 'Ahava ben Primo'.

She was anxious to open what was before her; could it really be the writings of the father she had never known? But Lord Aquila surveyed her, reading her expressions as he removed the timepiece he kept in his waistcoat pocket, and without observing the hour, he wound it with his thin, awkward fingers.

He replaced the watch and sat himself in a dusty velvet chair opposite Lucy. Without breaking her gaze, he placed his hand on the book and pushed it across the table to her.

She looked up at him, looking for confirmation that she could take it. Aquila nodded in affirmation.

The paper felt fragile in her clammy hands. That she should now be holding something in her hands that once belonged to our father seemed so strange. The whole world, until recently so peaceful, so simple, seemed so strange to her now!

The cover was green, but now so faded that it was the shade of peppermint. She brushed her fingers over the area where the signature sat, perhaps hoping for some sensation of a life long departed.

She folded back the cover and looked down on the first jaundiced page. The paper was so thin, you could almost make out the writing on the reverse.

She read the title aloud, '"The Canticle of Raya",' and looked up at the old man. 'What is this?'

'It is a story that your father wrote for your mother.'

Lucy's face beamed. She loved stories.

'What sort of a story is it? Does it have a happy ending?'

'It is a love story, child. No love story ever has a happy ending.'

Thirty Nine

THE PONY I TRAVELLED ON had short legs and so our progress was slow. Not quite as slow as Innocent Quibble's on his steed, though. Carrying the hefty weight of my portly travelling companion was proving an onerous task for the poor creature, its legs occasionally buckling under the duress of the burden of a man who could not see his feet to cut his toe-nails over the mound of his belly.

Eventually, as our pace slowed to no more than an amble, the leader of our party gestured for Quibble to be taken from the animal. Quibble had no sooner wriggled his way off the pony's back than he was suddenly airborne as the leader took hold of his arm with one hand and effortlessly hauled the tubby solicitor onto the back of his own magnificent stallion.

As he journeyed through the air, Quibble emitted a high-pitched (and a little undignified) yelp, his rear end landing on the horse's rear end with a *plomp*. Startled, he blustered, 'Well, I never did...' before tailing off into an inaudible blather.

I struggled to suppress a giggle, and I noticed one or two of the soldiers (if indeed they were soldiers) who had until now been emotionless, exchange amused curls of the lips.

Our journey continued in silence. These soldiers (which again I call them, but as I looked around I saw no uniform or, come to think of it, any weapons) seemed never to speak, communicating only through a look, a movement of the eyes, a nod of the head, or a gentle sweep of the hand.

I wanted to ask them so much, and yet so in awe was I of their silent strength that I too kept my mouth closed.

Who were these men who kept us captive? Were we in fact captive at all?

The day wore on; hours and hours seemed to pass as our party drove through the thick undergrowth.

The rain was now a drizzle, and cold and exhausted, I began to lurch forward on the pony's back and drift into a welcoming sleep.

I AWOKE WITH A START as I felt the terrain beneath us change as sludgy wetlands became solid rock and we started to ascend a small but relatively steep incline.

It was now dark as we made our way up the hill. My pony lurched slightly to the left as we turned the corner.

The men now carried flaming torches to light our way and I caught glimpse of Quibble who sat astride the great horse that the leader rode with authority along the path.

Quibble's eyes were wide, his expression anxious as we made our way toward the peak of the path.

The leader slowed his horse as the party reached dense woodland and raised his hand to indicate for the others that they were to stop.

In a single, graceful movement, he swung from the horse, landing elegantly on two feet, before extending his hand to Quibble to aid him from the mighty stallion. Quibble also found his way to the ground, although 'graceful' and 'elegant' are two words I cannot use to describe his descent.

'We camp here,' the leader proclaimed, and immediately the company sprang into action, erecting small, roughly-hewn, but effective shelters with warm woollen blankets scattered beneath them.

One of our 'guards' silently ushered Quibble and me to a shelter propped against a thick tree trunk.

I contentedly slipped beneath the awning and under the soft blanket. Mr. Quibble looked around uncertainly, clutching his blanket high against his chest.

'I do not like this, Master Joshua. I do not like it at all.'

'We have been well treated, so far. I'm sure if they meant us ill, we would have known about it by now,' I reassured, trying to convince myself that we were safe.

But the solicitor was not to be swayed. 'There is something in the eyes of these men; a deep, dark secret... It frightens me.'

'We are in the Kaharian, Mr. Quibble. Surely all men here are fundamentally good?'

'Of that I cannot be sure; and in any case, even if they are, as you say fundamentally good' – his voice dropped to a whisper – 'bear in mind, they may not take kindly to the mission on which we are set, which the guardians of the Kaharian may view as fundamentally un-good, that is to say, bad.'

Having exhausted himself in his fretful rambling, I asked the only question I could think of: 'Then what must we do?'

'We must escape.'

HAVING CONTINUED OUR CONVERSATION in hushed tones for some little while longer, it was decided we should get some rest and wait until the company was asleep before attempting to slip away into the forest.

Being dark, we could not know how much cover the forest would provide (if it was in fact a forest rather than simply a small clump of trees) or, indeed, where our flight might lead us, but Quibble's sense of foreboding overwhelmed him so that he felt we had little choice.

So it was with a gentle hand on the shoulder that I was stirred from a pleasant slumber by the sweating lawyer whose dark-circled eyes indicated he had not travelled to the land of nod for even a minute.

'The camp is quiet, Joshua. It is time. I have taken some water and bread, but now let us be gone from this place and these strange men.'

As quietly as I could, I pulled the cover from my body and rose, trying not to rustle the dry mattress of small twigs and leaves upon which I had slept.

Quibble was already up and looking twitchily left and right as he handed me a small bag with provisions for our journey.

We were at the very edge of the camp, and we inched our way forward into the woodland. Quibble's movements were edgy and uncharacteristically agile as he darted from tree to tree, taking cover against the thick trunks of the ancient oaks. I simply followed him, keeping my eyes wide open for anyone who might spot our attempted flight.

Soon we found ourselves a few hundred metres from the camp and at this point we abandoned our furtive zig-zagging movements and broke into a straight run across the uneven forest floor.

I glanced back and saw lamps were now lit at the camp and the men stood in a line looking after us – they had seen us!

And yet they made no movement.

Quibble had seen this too, but the lack of pursuit did not ease him. 'Hurry!' he insisted in a sharp whisper. 'We must away from here.'

Our short legs seemed quite well suited to our cross-country course and the uneven surfaces. The density of the forest would have made our route impassable for men on horseback, and after a period of flat-out sprinting, we allowed our pace to slacken, growing more confident that we were not being followed.

Unfortunately, even our slower pace did not allow us to be alert to what was ahead: as the forest came to an abrupt halt, I had the sudden sensation of falling.

FORTY

LUCY CAREFULLY TURNED THE PAGES of the delicate book, her fingers trembling as she did so, her eyes scanning the words.

The story was clearly written over some time as the handwriting and the inks that were used varied in places. The words were simple, perhaps her father wasn't much older than her when he wrote it, but the longing and the love lifted from the page like fine perfume.

'This is beautiful!' Lucy exclaimed as she continued to try to take in every line, her head not lifting from the book.

'Your father was a romantic. He saw the beauty in all things. And your mother was beauty itself.'

'They must have loved each other very much.'

Aquila didn't stir at this, but Lucy was not finished: 'Grandfather? Have you ever loved someone?'

He looked at her quizzically with eyebrow raised, and then threw his head back imperiously and gave a snort. 'This word... *love*, which some may call divine, may be resident in other men, but not in me...' He started to trail off as though his mind had suddenly turned to something else. 'Not in me.'

He suddenly started from his reverie, 'There is no such thing as love. There is only power.'

Lucy stood her ground (or at least sat her ground as she remained on her chair). 'I do not believe that. I believe that love is a real thing.'

'You may believe what you wish, child. Love is a wicked, false trick of the mind that only serves to weaken a man. I have no love, no loyalty for anyone but myself. That is all there is.'

Lucy looked at him unblinking, though her eyes were moist with sadness for the abject pain she felt for the absence of love in the man she saw before her.

'Nonetheless, Grandfather, I do love you.'

FORTY ONE

I DON'T KNOW IF YOU HAVE EVER FALLEN, but it is the oddest sensation. At first, a moment of unreality as your brain too slowly gets the message from your feet that all is not as it should be. Where is the ground beneath you? Then as you compute this message, a moment of panic as your mind and your limbs start to scramble for something to grasp hold of.

Having failed to locate a stray branch of finger-nail-wide outcrop on the rock to clasp onto with my flailing arms, on this occasion, I felt my upper body tip back and suddenly my eyes were staring up at the stars. I was conscious that I was screaming but I could not hear myself as my mind seemed to shut down all but the essential functions.

My screaming stopped and I closed my mouth as something in my mind told me that impact was close.

With a searing jolt I hit, and was suddenly under, the water. Immediately stunned by the crushing force of my landing, and feeling momentarily as though my head had come clean away from the rest of my body, my legs began to kick out, my arms began to claw through the water to get to the surface. But where was the surface! What was up, what was down? All became a blur as I struggled for my senses. As the current took me, I pounded into rock after rock. All the air in my lungs had been forced out by my landing and all I knew was that I needed to breathe. Then adrenaline and the lack of air made my mind whirr until all went black.

My head broke through the water and I came round to find myself being carried at some speed along a narrow, rocky ravine.

The boulders that dotted the course of the waterway sent waves crashing one way and the other. The chances of me not being pulverised against the monoliths seemed incredibly slim, and as my mind raced I decided that my best chance was, rather than be dashed against them, to try to hold onto one.

I didn't have time to ponder the possible insanity of what I was to attempt, so I spread my limbs wide to try to grab hold of something, anything!

I heard the crack of my small body clatter against the cold, slippery surface. Blood rushed to my brain as excruciating pain surged from my wrists and my ribs, but crucially, I held on, my fingers curved like talons gripping at the surface.

With the little purchase I had, I hauled myself up – the pain from my wrists shooting up my arms almost making me lose my grip, but somehow I was atop the rock and began to scuttle toward the bank with a combination of my feet and rear end.

The pain became unbearable and as I reached a small area of lush grass, I vomited before lying back on the floor (thankfully avoiding the pool of sick!) and looking up at the sky.

Day was breaking but the overwhelming pain made the blood pump in my skull. My eyelids became heavy and I shut them tight against the agony I felt.

Then all was still and I slipped into unconsciousness.

Forty Two

You are my North, my South, my East, my West,
And you are all the seasons of my year.
With you, I feel I can be the best,
With you I laugh when I am close to tears.
When I fall down, you lift me up again.
You are my light when dark is all around.
When I am hurt, you take away my pain,
Without complaint, without a single sound.
Your eyes blaze with love I have never seen.
Your lips sing songs as soft as summer breeze.
You give me strength when I just want to scream,
When I am afraid you put me at my ease.
My heart remains the same whate'er you do.
You are my day, my night, my life. You are you.

LUCY PUT THE BOOK DOWN on the table as she finished reading aloud, tears budding in her eyes.

'It is the most beautiful thing I have ever read!' she exclaimed, overwhelmed by emotion.

'It is saccharine, vomit-inducing piffle!' retorted Aquila, He saw in Lucy's eyes that his harsh words hurt her, and more softly, he added, 'Each to their own, of course. I am sure your father... tried hard.'

It is true, in the time that has passed, I have been fortunate to read many great poets – Teddy Devere is perhaps my favourite – and my father's jottings are not worthy of mention in the annals of great literature. The words were, however, sincere and they certainly wooed my mother!

Lucy wanted to know more and so she pressed, 'How did my parents meet?'

'They were promised to each other from birth. Your grandmother was human. In fact this house belonged to her family, before I made some... modifications.'

'Did you love my grandmother?'

'I have already answered that, I believe. You do have some foolishly romantic notions, girl. Your grandmother was very beautiful and she bore me a son. That is as far as my connection to her went. I felt nothing.

'Anyway, you distract me. So, your parents were promised to each other. A good family of some wealth of your grandmother's acquaintance gave birth to a delightful young girl, not long after your father arrived. It was a good match and would secure the fortunes of the Kerioth estate.

'I know such things are not smiled upon now by romantic idealists, such as yourself, who believe in clichéd fantasies about knights in shining armour sweeping flaxen-haired maidens off of their feet! Money, power and extending the family line are the only things that truly matter.'

'But my parents did love each other, nonetheless.'

'As fate would have it, through their childhood they eventually came to share a type of kinship, which you, poor deluded fool, refer to by that frightful word.

'They grew up together, and by the time they were your age, they were near inseparable. I believe it is around that period that your father began to write this story.

'They were married, happily by all accounts, and before long you and Joshua came into this world.

'Then things began to change as the spiritual battle for the Kaharian began.

'The humans were at first reasonably unaffected by the goings on in that realm, separated by time and dimension.'

'What happened?' Lucy enquired moving closer.

'I do not wish to speak of that now. However, many of those who were cast out wreaked havoc on earth for some time. We were defeated in battle, but we would take as many of the Pidaja's beloved humans with us as we could. Those lost souls you will have seen outside the castle at night, each one of them was slain by my enchantments, dead but not dead, suspended between earth and the Kaharian, so that they might know the dammed purgatory I must endure.

'Unsurprisingly, the villagers around these parts did not take kindly to their kith and kin falling prey to the nefarious curse of an old daemon, and yet I was untouchable. My favourite way to kill was to curse them with visions and hallucinations. I drove them mad, until they ran in front of a horse and cart or jumped from a bridge or drowned themselves in the lake. I killed them without laying a finger upon them. So neat, so clean. So wicked!'

He laughed the cruellest laugh it is possible to imagine, seemingly drunk on his own evil.

Lucy sat, stunned into silence by these revelations, but Primo Aquila was not done yet. 'And so it was, when your parents rode into the village, leaving you with the ghastly Miss Tibbs, coming in perfect peace to try to reason with the daemon in the castle, the mob mentality set in.

'Fools that the villagers were, they thought that beating and torturing your parents would somehow make me show mercy on them – "bring me to my senses".'

'Your parents were strung up like animals in the marketplace when Picardo summoned me to attend. Your mother, poor soul, had breathed her last, but your father, brave as he was, held on although every bone was broken and tears of blood trickled down his cheeks.'

Lucy was now fighting back tears as she also tried to fight back the images that coursed through her mind. 'And did you try to nurse my father?'

'Oh no, dear, I did the only kind and fatherly thing I ever did for him. I shot him dead.'

The room was silent. What passed through Lucy's mind at that moment I can only imagine, although she displayed nothing of the rage that I still feel these many years on simply writing these words.

'You did what?'

'I shot him. Dear girl, it was the only kind thing to do. He would not have survived the journey back to the castle. I ended his pain.'

'But you can do magic. You could have saved him!'

'My dear, my particular gifting by this stage more concerned the ending of life rather than the giving or prolonging thereof. I make no apology for my actions.'

Lucy placed her head on her hands on the table, her shoulders rising and falling in rapid motion as she sobbed.

Our grandfather looked at her with incredulity at the pain she felt, and yet something – yes, perhaps *something* – flickered behind his eyes, somehow wishing that he could feel something other than hate.

FORTY THREE

If I'm to die, I'll fight to my last breath,
And you must promise for me you'll not cry.
I'm not afraid though I am facing death,
For our love lives on, should I live or die.
Dark comes and life seems to slip away,
But my soul lives on to love another day.

DAWN WAS BREAKING THROUGH the huge window at the
end of the library. Lucy had been reading all night, with every
page, every paragraph, every stanza, mourning the parents we
never knew.

To her surprise, she had had a constant companion through
the night: as the light angled in through the thick glass, there she
saw him silhouetted against the daybreak.

Stooped in his chair, he looked out to the world beyond as he
had done for hours, not speaking, not moving, save for the
occasional drumming of his long fingers on the top of his walking
cane.

Every muscle in Lucy's body had stiffened from her night
crouched over a desk reading by the light of a single lamp. She
stood and straightened, her hair falling loose as those tightened
muscles unravelled from their coiled state back to their natural
positions.

Quietly, she started to make her way toward the window,
pausing here and there where the title of a book caught her eye;
and then, something she had missed before, although quite how

she missed it was unknown, as it dominated the left hand corner of the room nearest the window.

Elegantly carved in oak, a tall, thick-set bookstand in the shape of an eagle, a leafed branch between its talons.

So tall it was that there were three small stone steps up, which Lucy now ascended, although to her disappointment she found no book there. Instead there was a rectangular outline of darker wood, the rest of the stand having been bleached by the sun.

Having almost lost her voice from crying, Lucy now cleared her throat, and the old daemon by the window turned his head a few degrees as she now spoke. 'The book that once rested here, Grandfather, where is it?'

Lord Aquila's reply was even in tone but cold. 'You will not find that pack of lies in this house. It has been cast into the fire many years since.'

'Whatever was it?'

'It was your father's copy of the scripture.'

PART FOUR

Akeldama

FORTY FOUR

AS I CAME BACK TO CONSCIOUSNESS I was aware that my eyes would not open, but I could hear, and what a curious sound it was that I heard.

The voice was unmistakably that of Innocent Quibble, the portly solicitor who was my travelling companion, but the tongue in which he spoke was distinctly foreign to me.

'Esh cere mata bura nei. Em kerem a tana bethlaka pura mea.'

He continued on. I could feel his pudgy hand firmly but tenderly pressed against my forehead.

This went on for some time and Quibble was persistent in his strange incantation.

'Neka bura, neka bura allomi. Teka kerem abaneithon sensei chillagi bura. Neka bura!'

At these last words my eyes opened and I felt myself gasp in a deep breath of life.

Quibble staggered back in wonder and a smile shone from his round, toadish face.

I did not move, I could not move. As the feeling returned to my body, so did the pain. My ribs, my arms, the tips of my fingers all screamed with hurt.

I heard the water of the ravine rushing alongside the grassy bank where I lay, but could not turn to see anything other than the mottled grey of the sky above.

Then, on the periphery of my sight I sensed a movement and a shadow.

A shadow, and yet *not* a shadow, for whatever came now in my direction seemed to cast a light rather than block the light.

The shape that was cast was not human, but what was it?

Quibble had backed away and was silent. And then, there, just inches from my face, there was another face.

A deer.

The deer looked deep within me, with its searching, deep chestnut-coloured eyes, its long eyelashes giving a sense of feminine, almost motherly, reassurance.

Then suddenly the face was gone and the sky returned.

I felt a nestling against my chest, and the sense that the deer was rubbing her face against me. With shocking suddenness there was a cold, stabbing pain in my ribs – momentary but intense – before... nothing. The pain had gone. The deer rubbed against my arms – the same cold stab before the warmth of relief.

I raised my restored arms to the skies and saw the deer lick the blood from my battered fingers and the wounds close themselves and heal instantly with not a scar or blemish to be seen.

The deer now lowered her head again to mine and licked my cheek.

I had never felt such warmth; such love. The deer nudged my cheek and I lifted my head and with that, she darted into the trees.

FORTY FIVE

SPRING WAS STARTING TO COME to Kerioth. Flowers began to open their buds and butterflies fluttered by as Lucy walked toward the headland cliff.

The dewy grass brushed against her sandaled feet as she made her way in a light, pastel cotton dress, a jug of ginger ale and two glasses in her hands.

Primo Aquila, as he so often did in these recent days, sat staring at the sea beyond. His cruel eyes, reddened and unblinking as they looked out at the waves thundering against the rocks below.

He started when he heard the chinking of glasses as Lucy approached. He turned and smiled his twisted smile.

Some days had passed since Lord Aquila had confessed that he had shot our father.

From that time their conversations had been civil but brief; each taking their meals separately, perhaps both knowing the hurt that re-exploring the subject might cause.

So they went about life, such as life was, quietly for those days: Lucy poring over books, Aquila staring at the water and incessantly winding his watch.

His smile now, though, as he gazed on her pretty face was genuine.

My sister was so often the peacemaker in our own squabbles as children, always knowing the right time and the right gesture to put a disagreement or a hurt to rest, and now with a jug of ginger ale on a sunny morning, she found warmth in the reception she received.

As she looked at our grandfather, she nervously bit her top lip as was her habit before she spoke. 'I thought you might like something to drink, Grandfather?'

He nodded for her to join him on the bench upon which he sat, carved from the trunk of a tree. 'That is very kind. I would be delighted.'

Lucy poured the cold, frothing nectar into the glasses and handed one to the old daemon. He bowed his head in quiet thanks and turned back to the sea. Lucy too turned her gaze.

Quiet fell between them as they took in the view, took in the sun, and took in the awkwardness of the moment.

'My dear, I know you think me very cruel in my words and my actions...'

Lucy looked anxiously away, fearing some new pain about to be delivered. Aquila checked himself, noticing her reaction and he softened his voice. 'But you must understand there is no hope for me. I have no love in my heart. I have been denied human emotion. I am a daemon.'

Lucy straightened her back and calmly turned her head to see the grizzled, wizened face staring back at her. As she spoke, her tone was measured but full of earnest intensity.

'Grandfather, I know but too well what and who you are, and some of the many evils you have done. But it was not always so. You were an angel of the Kaharian!'

With that he stood sharply and spat, 'Do not use that word!'

Lucy maintained poise as she responded calmly, 'But that is your true self. I know who you are, but I want to know who you were.'

Her words left the hell-hound speechless. He looked aimlessly at the ground beneath, his eyes scrunched up, face wrinkled in deep concentration trying to remember who he was... or trying to forget.

Lucy pressed again, deliberately aiming to provoke a response. 'You were an angel of the Kaharian!'

The daemon collapsed back into his seat, dropping his cane as he held his head in his hands. 'I... I was.'

'Then tell me about the Primo Aquila you were born as.'

'I was not born, child, not in any conventional sense. Not as you were born of your mother and father. I was imagined into existence, a puff of breath from the Pidaja's lips forming in the air and given glorious flight.'

He trailed off as teardrops grew in the corner of his eyes.

'Tell me about him, that Primo Aquila who could fly.'

He studied my sister long and hard, noting the steel and the compassion in her bright, green eyes.

'Very well.'

FORTY SIX

'QUICKLY, LET US FOLLOW!' Quibble exclaimed gathering himself. I staggered onto my feet, tottering slightly having been lying down for an unknown period of time, my head still swimming slightly, although my body felt full of health and energy.

We dashed into the woodrow, catching a glimpse of the rear quarters of the doe that had been my miraculous healer.

The deer was fast and agile, but the wood was not so dense with trees and so while we were not able to keep pace, we were at least able to keep sight of the lithe creature.

As I sprinted, I panted, 'Why are we following?'

Wheezing, the solicitor replied, 'I do not yet know.'

It was not the most reassuring response to hear in this strange land and yet we continued our pursuit unquestioningly.

Ahead of us the forest came to an end and we saw the deer stop. We continued to run and eventually we were within a few metres, when suddenly, the doe dissolved into the air.

We found ourselves stood on the edge of a great plain. The cracked earth looked very much like the plain upon which we had entered this Kaharian realm. Surely we had not come a full circle, to return to where we had started?

I put this proposition to Quibble. His reply was ambiguous as he gazed out over the endless landscape with an ashen expression: 'I only wish it were, Joshua.'

'Then where are we?'

'This is Akeldama. Please be careful to watch your step, dear boy, making every effort not to walk on the cracks.'

The answer puzzled me but didn't draw response, instead I decided to keep my counsel and follow Quibble's presumably knowledgeable advice.

We walked for some time, our eyes not meeting as we kept our gaze on our feet below us. Eventually, I spoke:

'Mr. Quibble, as I was lying by the river, I heard you speaking some strange words over me. What was it you were saying?'

'I was praying, Joshua. I was appealing to the Pidaja to see you safe; and he did so. It was, however, a foolish thing to do.'

Every night when I was younger, Tibbs had prayed with Lucy and me; thanking the Pidaja for the day that had passed and asking for protection for the night to come, but never in that strange language.

'The language you spoke...'

'I do not know, Joshua. I just opened my mouth and that is what came out. The deer, I am certain, was the miraculous answer to those curious words, though. A thought which fills me with joy and with fear.'

'Why fear?'

'Because if the Pidaja heard my prayer, then he truly knows our every thought, feeling and movement. He knows we are here and he knows why we are here.'

I thought on this for a moment. 'And yet he does not stop us. In fact, if the deer was sent to heal, it is almost as though he is helping us.'

As I said this, I stopped walking and looked up at Quibble. He then turned and looked at me, or rather he looked to my feet.

I didn't look down initially, but felt a warm, moist sensation in my shoes. I cast my eyes downwards to see blood seeping from the cracks in the earth and into my shoes, slowly rising, now nearly up to the top of my shoes.

'Joshua, I want you to remain quite calm, but to keep walking briskly, making every effort not to step on the cracks further.'

I extracted my sodden feet from the gloopy, crimson puddle and started to plant one foot after the other, marching onwards, but now with every step, the earth seemed to crumble below my feet, and then Quibble's feet, and turn to viscous red liquid.

Our pace quickened, but as it did so, so the cracks opened wider, the earth splitting, the crimson river swelling, threatening to burst its banks into a torrent.

'Run, Joshua!' yelled my companion as I struggled to pull my feet through the heavy substance, losing my left shoe in the process.

'Mr. Quibble! I am scared!'

'Quickly, my boy! Just keep going, keep moving your legs, do not stop!'

I tried to wade through the stream of blood that now covered my ankles.

Quibble, too, was struggling and started to panic as his fat legs became immobile. He began to scream. I began to scream, and then from nowhere, a voice, silent and yet booming in my mind: 'Be still!'

Then the sky turned to black.

FORTY SEVEN

'YES, I WAS, AS YOU SAY, AN... ANGEL.' The word seemed to stick in his throat.

'You lived in the Kaharian? Where you sent Joshua?'

'I did. I did. I was handsome then, my child. I was not as you see angels in books, cloaked in white. No, I was cloaked in light! The radiance of the angels was something to behold, and something to be feared.

'I was a sentinel, a watchman. At the creation of the earth I was there watching, observing, carrying out the tasks assigned to me.

'And then humans were created, and I observed them. I observed their wickedness and their disobedience to the one who created them, and the creator's mystifying, infuriating patience with their deceit and corruption.

'I was not the only one who saw this indulgence as weakness. We, who had served so faithfully from the beginning, were now side-lined in favour of a chosen people who were born stupid and evil.'

Lucy remained calm but firm. 'Do you include me in that assessment?'

'You may think you can draw a retraction with your pretty looks and honeyed words, young lady, but you have no idea what I talk of: the pain of those who had been faithful and good, obedient and worthy – born of his very breath, and then treated like dogs to try to salvage the failed experiment of humankind.

'Yes, I include you in that assessment and every one of your wretched race. I curse you all.

'I soon grew sick of my lowly status, when once I had known power and greatness in the Kaharian. I longed with all my heart to have that power and greatness restored to me and have him smile on me again as once he did.

'My discontent was unnoticed by the Pidaja, but not by another. One I would go on to call my master.'

'Who was he?' Lucy enquired.

'The most beautiful of all the angels in my view: the Morning Star.

'He was truly great and truly powerful; an archangel. One of the closest circle to the throne of thrones. And yet he saw, as I had, the insanity of the experiment.

'He started to find other supporters in the choir of angels, but also among the humans. The Pidaja, who they had been told was so good, so loving, had let many of them suffer in abject conditions.

'Many of the humans began to wonder if the Pidaja even existed, but they were naught to the Morning Star. No, the humans he wanted by his side when the time came were those who actively hated the Pidaja. Hate, you see, is a powerful, powerful emotion.

'We simply ensured the people suffered, that their prayers went unanswered, and so the anger festered inside them – until the time came.'

Lucy sat spellbound at the tale, and was scared of the bitterness with which Aquila spoke.

'What happened?'

'As with all displays of pride and ambition against the throne, we were brought to our knees. There was a fearsome battle over many centuries in the Kaharian, though for just a few years here on earth. Fire and brimstone rained down on the unfaithful, while the "righteous" were saved.

'The Morning Star was cast into the fiery pit for all eternity, and we, the shamed foot soldiers of the rebellion, were chained.'

'You were put in prison?' Lucy questioned.

Primo Aquila slowly pulled the pocket watch from his waistcoat. 'No, my dear, we were chained by time.'

The sun glistened on the gold links of the thick chain that attached the timepiece to our grandfather's navel. He was pensive now.

'Growing old is a terrible thing, Lucy, when you know there is nothing on the other side of death for you. I, who served for millennia, am now reduced to a scared old fool, trembling, waiting for the candle to fizzle out and darkness to fall. The immortal made mortal.

'I would rather he had struck me down there and then for my crimes, of which I confess my guilt. But to make me sit and wait, watching myself die; my every movement becoming more feeble and unnatural, my mind becoming weaker and slower... That is the cruelty of the Pidaja. It was not enough to make me mortal and kill me; I was made to wallow in my own mortality and see my life just ebb away to nothing.

'Unless your brother returns...'

FORTY EIGHT

'I LIKE TO COME HERE, CHILD, to this cliff top. I like to watch the waves and the tides. They are the immortal timelessness I want to know again.

'Like time they are both constant and constantly changing. The waves bring life and they bring death.

'Oh, to return to the time before time began, before man sought order and structure to the world that was made for neither. There was only one law, the covenant, and that was all that was needed.

'Now, men race everywhere, their heads lowered, seeing nothing of the world around them. Children still in their cradles, routined and scheduled. Time takes life from the living and will drive each man to his death with its incessant, mechanical beat.

'Once there was a time when you could close your eyes here on earth and you could hear the beauty of the Kaharian: the chirruping of birds, the gushing of water from eternal springs, the hum of bees collecting pollen. Now the only sound left in the world is the constant tick of our own death march.'

He breathed deeply as he contemplated his watch, 'And now the march slows for me. The drum's tempo slackening until soon it will beat no more.'

Lucy put her delicate hand on his arm.

'Joshua will be back. If there is anyone I know, though I do not know many people, who is brave enough and determined enough to succeed in this quest, it is my brother.'

Lord Aquila tried to snort in derision, although even that had an air of resignation, 'It is a fool's mission. I have sent your brother and that buffoon of a solicitor to their deaths. They may already be dead, and with that, my own death will not be long in coming.'

Lucy looked out to the ocean as she gripped onto her grandfather's arm. 'I still believe.'

There was quiet, but for the waves washing against the outcrop of jagged rocks below.

Lucy changed tack now. 'Grandfather, if you die, I will die also.'

He looked at her incredulously. 'Of course you won't child!'

'But you said...'

'I say a lot of things. I have told you before – I tell lies. Sometimes even I can't remember what the truth is any more, so deep and complex is the web of deceit I have spun; but no, no you will not die when I do.'

Lucy trembled at this, having prepared herself for the possibility of imminent death. 'But what kind of a life will I have? All the ones I love have gone: Josh, Miss Tibbs... you...'

The words hung in the air for a moment, before he replied, 'You will have the life you choose for yourself, Lucy. Time will eventually take all mortals, but you can choose to stay locked away, mourning for those whom you grieve, or you can live your life.

'Now, pass me some more of that delicious ginger ale.'

FORTY NINE

THE BLACKNESS OF THE SKY is hard to describe to you, but it went beyond an absence of colour and light; it was as though life was sucked out of the sky in those brief moments. An abyss.

I found myself aware that I was now within touching distance of Innocent Quibble; I reached out to him and he held my hand tightly.

There were no words to be spoken, I am not even sure sound was possible in the black hole we now found ourselves; and then, we were off our feet, flying, spiralling through the air.

The wind was knocked from my lungs as we span, gaining height all the time, then flipped upside down before suddenly we felt our feet firm on solid rock.

The blackness dissolved and daylight appeared. I shielded my eyes from the bright light, as I adjusted from the darkness.

When I gained clarity, I looked around me and was startled to find my feet inches from the edge of a sheer drop of hundreds of feet.

Dizzied, I tottered backwards from the cliff and into the arms of Mr. Quibble.

'What happened?' I blurted, feeling queasy from the motion of the unusual journey we had just made.

'I have little notion, young fellow. Suffice to say I feel somewhat happier here, barren though it is, than on the plains of Akeldama.'

I looked out over the valley that was laid out before us, the sun glistening against the vast golden rocks which formed irregular pillars as far as the eye could see. It was the most breathtaking view I had encountered to that day, and there have been very few to rival it since.

'What exactly is Akeldama?'

'It may not surprise you to know it is "the field of blood", although how it came to claim that name is a rather longer story.'

I felt boldly curious. 'It's a story I'd like to hear.'

'Let us get out of this beating sun and I will endeavour to tell it.'

We started to trek on a long, zig-zagging path that began to take us down into the valley floor.

Within what felt like a furlong or so, Quibble was sweating profusely. Thankfully, there was a small cavern in the rock which provided some shelter from the heat of the day.

Quibble sat on a little ledge, fanning himself furiously, trying unsuccessfully to find some cool breeze in the still, arid air.

I lay on the cool floor of the cavern. I looked down at my feet, one shoe-less and stained red with blood, but not from my own veins.

I revived our earlier exchange. 'Please tell me about Akeldama.'

'Ah, yes. Now, you remember all I told you about my meeting with your grandfather?'

'Yes, of course.'

'Well, as disenchantment grew on earth with the Pidaja, so it grew a thousand-fold in the Kaharian.

'Lucian Strafe, your grandfather, and many others openly revolted and sought to overthrow the Pidaja, believing his love of humans was a weakness. There was a great battle on the earth and in the Kaharian, two battlefields in parallel, battles in two dimensions. There was much bloodshed.

'Firstly, many who had loyally attended the temple and continued to worship the Pidaja just disappeared from their beds one night as though they had never been there, many of my own followers and friends among them. Lucian, the deceiver, used this as evidence to the mob that either the Pidaja did not exist or that he cared so little that he had allowed many of his followers to be exterminated in cold blood.

'It was nonsense of course; at the time I suspected that Lucian and his gang of mercenaries had simply murdered them for their own ends.

'I am now of the belief that the Pidaja actually took his faithful flock into his care, away from the battle.

'There were riots in the streets, temples were burnt to cinders. A great war began. It lasted several years, encompassing nations. Brother fought brother. Allies broke their bonds and turned fire upon their own. They were but pawns in a tussle for control of a far greater prize. Many lost their lives, a number of them by my own hand, I regret to say.'

He faltered as he recalled the events.

'Here in the Kaharian, the battle was even fiercer; it was the battle for the control of all time and space. Angels in bitter conflict with their kin; in battle their immortality was void and many fell from both sides.

'The rebellion was annihilated, crushed. Lucian, the manipulator, had stayed well out of harm's way in battle, but now there was no hiding place as he was forced to bow before the throne of thrones; his generals with him, your grandfather foremost among them.

'The Morning Star was cast to the pit to burn for all time, alive but with no life other than to try to manipulate and twist truth.

'Akeldama is the field where the great battle took place; under its surface runs the blood of those who fell. It is also the gateway to the pit.

'It is his nature. Where a crack appears in our lives, in our personalities, our habits, our relationships, he seeps into it, just as he was trying to pull us through the cracks in the land. He was defeated, but he will try to rise again. His all-consuming pride will not allow him to rest until the world of men falls to him.'

By now I was upright, and shuddered in absolute terror at what I heard.

'My greatest fear, Master Joshua, is that your grandfather's scheme may bring that day of darkness closer than we can conceive.'

I spoke now. 'Mr. Quibble, the thing I don't understand is that you are an intelligent man – Mr. Picardo, too – and yet despite knowing the evil that my grandfather has engaged in, you have not fled from his service.'

Quibble looked to the floor, embarrassed that a twelve-year-old child had exposed such a blatant hypocrisy.

'No, no I haven't. He saved our lives, Joshua. After the battle ended on earth, the authorities started their hunt to bring the perpetrators to justice.

'Picardo and I were tracked down to a cottage in the mountains north of Kerioth. The mob circled the perimeter, torches aflame, and they set light to the building.

'And then, when death seemed certain, our guardian angel flew in to our rescue. We were borne on his magnificent wings and carried to safety at the castle.

'It was the last time I saw your grandfather with wings. When he returned to Kerioth, he was... well, he was much changed, in appearance and attitude.

'As for the reason I am here now, Lord Aquila has promised that if we succeed in this matter, he will cure my son of his affliction. He is the only one who possibly can.'

'Do you believe he will keep his promise?'

'I know not, Master Joshua, but it is the only hope my dear wife and I have.'

Quibble now looked out and saw the sun was dimming in the sky.

'I think it is cool enough to walk on now, Joshua. Let us seek food and shelter from the night.'

With that we made our way in silence.

FIFTY

ALTHOUGH THE SUN WAS BEGINNING TO FADE in the sky, the dry heat was still intense as we made progress down the gentle slope toward the valley's bottom.

Each footstep kicked up a small cloud of dust from the baked soil.

Our throats felt just as parched as the land and thirst and heat began to take a dizzying grip on us both.

With time being such an arbitrary thing in this strange land, there was no knowing when last we drank. Maybe when we were captured by the herdsmen? But how long ago was that?

I imagine I swallowed some water as I was plunged into the river, although that hardly felt reviving.

Oh, for my thirst to be quenched now!

And then, as we rounded a bend in the path, there was a sight spectacular to the eye at any time, but to the weary, dried-out traveller, it was a sight of pure bliss!

There, barely a furlong in the distance, at the foot of the hill was a lush, green patch of land, water spouting from the rocks, flowers in full bloom, and the sound of birdsong.

Tiredness was set aside as we sprinted the remainder of the way into the cool mist of the water's spray, plunging our hands into the refreshing pools that had formed.

Quibble sat by the edge of one pool, and removed his shoes, socks and garters before dipping his toes in. He gave a little playful yelp of surprise as the cold water tickled his throbbing webbed feet.

I lay in the long grass, delighting in its soft embrace, and just rolling back and forth, watching the blades flatten and spring back as I passed over them.

Then the sounds of flowing water and birds became strangely muted, as though my head was underwater. The noises had become muffled and seemed as though they were far away, although I hadn't moved. Another sound followed, this one so close it was almost as though it was inside my brain.

Mr. Quibble heard it too for I heard his voice, although it was distorted as though he were speaking in slow-motion.

The sound in my ears was simultaneously shrill and resonant, both dissonant and harmonious. A sound more extraordinary, more captivating than any I had known. It seemed to lift my head and carry me on wings, like an eagle soaring above the clouds.

It was as though I was drunk on music. All my other senses seemed dull and slow, all I could take in was this heavenly sound.

I was suddenly aware that I was now on my feet, and those feet were moving toward a deep cave in the side of the hill. The music still poured into me and I was its slave; it drew me into the dark of the cave, Quibble beside me, perhaps drawing us closer to its source.

Where this music led, I surely would follow.

FIFTY ONE

ALTHOUGH SPRING WAS UPON KERIOTH, the evenings were still cool as the breeze whipped across the lake.

So it was that the fire was lit and warm tea replaced iced ginger ale as the drink of choice as my sister and grandfather talked into the evening.

Their conversation had taken a lighter turn through the afternoon as they discussed the flowers and plants in the gardens of the great house.

My grandfather was intrigued by Lucy's extensive knowledge of flora and fauna, and she by his. Although by his own admission, it was Picardo who tended the gardens, he was at pains to remind her that he had been present when many of the flowers and trees she so admired were given life and named in a garden even fairer than his own.

As the light began to fade, Lucy had the old daemon trying to make daisy chains before he lost his temper as his spindly fingers attempted to thread the stems. However, prior to that, she was sure she caught a look in his eye, a look of pleasure, of happiness.

Picardo poured steaming tea and put the cup on a table at Lucy's side, where there was already a sticky bun on a plate, begging to be devoured.

Lord Aquila poked at the fire with his stick.

'That will be all, thank you, Picardo. You may retire for the night.'

'Thank you, my Lord.' The servant gave a small bow of the head and made his way from the room.

Grandfather continued to prod at the flames, and they spat back little sparks which made him startle slightly. Lucy observed him with patience and wisdom as he did this for several minutes.

'The fire interests you, does it not, Grandfather?'

He surveyed her before answering, 'I have known the fire more than most. The fire of righteousness, the fire of ambition, the fire of hatred. Fire was my weapon, and was also my punishment.'

Lucy didn't ask for more information, and yet he volunteered it.

'You see, my dear. When the forces of the Morning Star were defeated in battle, those rebels that had survived were forced to bow before the throne of the Pidaja, and we were severely punished. The chain you know about, attached to us at the place where you humans have a "belly button". The pain when they, my own kin, inserted the chain was beyond your earthly comprehension, searing and unyielding, and yet worse was to come. Next they hacked off our wings and left only these stumps, bleeding and raw' – he pointed to the two protrusions on his back – 'before we were cast out, but not initially to earth. First to the pit of fire, where my master, the bright Morning Star, still burns.

'I was once beautiful, now I am deformed, unfinished, my skin charred and blackened by the eternal furnace.'

'But you escaped the fire?'

'No, not escaped. Only the Morning Star was condemned to spend eternity aflame. His generals, and I among them, were damned to purgatory – between the lofty skies and the bowels of the earth. For my pride and jealousy of humankind, I was condemned to be as one with them. I was made ordinary, when I had been extraordinary.'

'Tell me about the Pidaja.'

He looked at her with a smirk of incredulity. 'You are not serious?'

'I am. Tibbs spoke to us of him, although she called him by another name. I think she called him "The Great Ian".'

Aquila threw his head back and shrieked with laughter. Uncontrollable gales of guffaws. Lucy looked at him nonplussed, and he came back to calm.

'I am sorry, my dear, that tickled me. No, not "The Great Ian" but "The Great I Am"! I mean, the arrogance of that title.'

'But the Pidaja is good?'

'Is the world free from suffering, child? Is it free from famine, and hardship and pain?'

'Well, no, it's not.'

'Then you have your answer. The Pidaja has dominion over these things and yet he brings destruction to the people he claims to love.'

'But people sometimes bring destruction on themselves, don't they, by disobeying the Pidaja, the Great I Am. I mean, yourself for instance...'

Lucy trailed off, knowing her tongue had perhaps run away with her a little, and she gulped hard as she prepared the expected torrent of anger that would undoubtedly be the consequence of her impertinence.

Yet the torrent never came. Primo Aquila just stared icily at the fire, pondered a moment, before muttering, barely audibly above the crackle of the flames, 'Perhaps you are right.'

FIFTY TWO·

I DON'T KNOW IF YOU HAVE EVER been enchanted; very possibly not as it does not occur all that often, but it is a quite peculiar experience.

You are fully aware of what is happening around you, although everything seems to be slowed, like putting a gramophone record on at the wrong speed. Although you see and hear what is happening, you are unable to control what is around you, and you are driven solely by a sight or a sound, and nothing and nobody will divert you from that.

In this particular instance it was a sound of course. It was the sound of a human voice and yet it was almost inhuman; too pure, too perfect to come from the lungs of a mere mortal. The words were indistinct to me, and still at the same time, they lifted my soul, raising my heart in praise.

By this time, that joyous sound was the only thing that guided us; we were now some distance into the cave and it was quite black.

We followed the sound of the voice, delirious in our pilgrimage to the source of this divine music, and then there ahead of us, emitting a low, faint light against the dark of the cave, was the unmistakable shape of... a deer!

I had no control over my body, it seemed to have developed quite a life of its own, but my heart pumped faster at the sight of that miraculous animal.

Alongside me, Quibble wibbled and wobbled, his considerable frame now illuminated dimly by the fair creature ahead.

Like automatons we followed in our hypnotic trance, until our senses were dazzled and confused by sudden light.

The music continued and was still magical, but I could feel my body again.

The room was large and circular, and stretched high with a domed, rocky ceiling. It was bathed with the light of a hundred torches, and filled with the sound of a hundred celestial voices; each of the owners of those voices stood, their hands raised toward the skies, their heads lifted high. We had seen the bodies of the voices before – they were the herdsmen we had escaped.

Innocent Quibble looked at me, eyes wide, and whispered, 'Let us leave this place, before we are noticed! This sound is witchcraft, I tell you!' But as he turned to scarper, I grabbed his thick forearm.

'No, let us stay!' Before I knew what I was doing, rather than hanging back and observing this strange assembly sing, at once with wild abandon and with perfect control, I found myself following the deer which unashamedly made its way through the throng toward a platform at the front, where several of the men sat playing a variety of instruments I had not seen before; some plucked with the fingers, some blown, some seemingly operating of their own accord with mere gestures enough to draw melodies of exquisite beauty from them. At the centre of these men stood the leader of the group we had encountered. He played an instrument that looked like the violin Lucy had been instructed in by Miss Tibbs, but there was no childish screeching. The man simply breathed upon the strings and they produced a sound that was achingly beautiful.

The doe approached the leader, and he stroked the deer's nose. Something astonishing then happened.

The doe backed up onto its hind legs and in an instant there was a swirl of colour and light and there stood a girl.

And what a girl she was! She was only a little older than I, simply dressed in a fawn-coloured tunic. Her hair was cut short and neatly tied back, but it was the lustre of her face and her deep brown eyes that, even from a distance, captured me instantly.

The music played on, but it was not that which held me in its spell any longer!

The girl or deer, whatever she was, looked my way now, and the leader followed her gaze and saw me; but I did not care, I just wanted to be closer to that lovely apparition!

The leader continued to play while keeping his eyes fixed on me, eventually bringing the band to a halt as I approached the platform on which they stood.

So taken was I, that I had quite forgotten about Innocent Quibble who was still squatting at the back, cowering out of sight, and so entranced was I, that I hadn't noticed that as the music stopped, the assembly's gaze was not now shooting enraptured glances at the sky, but was now turned on me.

I was now just feet away from the girl. I looked deep into her eyes, and she looked back at me.

Her lovely, fair eyebrows raised slightly, furrowing her brow inquisitively.

'Hello?'

I didn't blink, taken by those perfect teeth she flashed, framed by perfect, plump pink lips.

'Hi!' was all I could manage.

Her lip curled at the corner, and she gave a gentle laugh,

'It appears we have a guest, Father.'

Suddenly aware, my eyes turned now to the leader.

'Indeed. It is good to see you again, young man. Although you seem to be alone?'

'Oh no!' I replied. 'Mr. Quibble is right behind me.'

I turned to find him absent, before catching sight of him at the back of the room. The entire throng turned to where I was looking and Innocent Quibble gave a sheepish wave, seeming less than delighted to have been discovered.

FIFTY THREE

INNOCENT QUIBBLE NEEDED NO ESCORT as he made his way through the gathered herdsmen, walking with an awkward shuffle, acutely aware of a hundred pairs of eyes on his every movement.

He forced a pained smile to greet the blank faces that surveyed him. There was not a murmur in the room, just a small squeak of patent leather shoes treading the bare rock floor of the cavern.

The solicitor reached the front.

'Well, this is jolly isn't it?' he exclaimed with false gaiety.

'My friends, you are most welcome here. I give praise that you are returned to us. We thought we had lost you!'

Quibble spluttered, his second chin wobbling as he spoke, 'My good fellow, you apprehended us and took us as your prisoners! And you have the gall to call us "friends"?'

The leader's face remained unmoved.

'Did we bind you or give chase when you fled?'

Quibble looked puzzled. 'Well, no, no you didn't, but...'

'You were never our captives. We sought only to assist you.'

'Well, I...'

'My name is Heman; this is my daughter Cara Lily, whom I believe you have met.'

'Yes, yes, we have met,' I answered, my eyes fixed on her. And she smiled at me. *She smiled at me!* Oh joy of joys!

Quibble still was flustered. 'And who are these, these farm boys?'

'These are my brothers, Mr. Quibble,' said Heman, 'we are the Sons of Korah.'

'Oh, I see,' Quibble came back, 'would it be terribly rude of me to say that name is not one that rings any bells? Should I have heard of you?'

'For many years, it was the blackest family name on the earth. Let us take some refreshment somewhere more intimate and we can talk further of the past, the present, and the future.'

Heman raised his hand to the assembly, and the crowd went their separate ways, some to other tunnels, others out in the direction we had arrived from, but each one in silence.

'They don't say very much, your brothers?'

Then Cara took my arm to usher me away and whispered, 'That too will all become clear to you.'

But the question had already faded from my mind at the delicacy and warmth of her touch. The blood rushed to my head and I felt a tingling in my cheeks. For certain, I was blushing.

Cara noticed and averted her gaze from mine, and I imagined, just for a moment, that she was blushing, too.

WE MOVED INTO A SMALL ANTECHAMBER off of the main cave, where we were invited to sit on rugs on the floor.

The room was lit and heated by a small fire, which caught Cara's eyes and made them sparkle.

I realise now that I am gushing, and so will endeavour to refrain from mentioning her sheer perfection. The truth is that even at that stage I was very much in love with her and I have not stopped loving her since.

We sat, the four of us – Quibble, Heman, Cara and I – in a square around the fire pit that was dug into the hard, golden rock.

Heman took an earthenware jug and poured an amber liquid into finely made goblets. He handed one to me, and I took a large swig of its contents.

I was thirsty. Although it had not been long since we had taken refreshment at the spring, my nervous excitement around Cara had made my mouth quite dry.

The liquid was cool in the mouth and yet warmed the gullet as it slid down, then forming a little cauldron of heat in my stomach, and while the nectar went straight to my tummy, its effects went directly to my head and I felt a slight giddiness.

'Go steady with that!' Heman advised. 'It is a potent mix for one of tender years.'

I watched Cara now as she delicately sipped at her cup, winking at me to show how it should be consumed. I followed her lead.

Quibble took a little nip from his goblet and gave a tip of the head in appreciation.

'I say! That is a very fine blend, sir. May I ask what it is?'

'It is made from crushed beetles and the intestinal fluids of a baby shemath' – Quibble swallowed hard in disgust, trying not to bring the liquid back up, wishing he had not asked the question – 'mixed with the hand pressed juice of a papaya... just to take the edge off it!' Heman finished. It might have been better if he had only told us that.

'Have you ever tried a papaya, Joshua?' Cara asked, her eyes wide.

'No, I don't think I have. I am not even sure what it is.' I then thought further. 'How do you know my name?'

Cara just laughed a tuneful laugh.

'Joshua,' her father picked up, 'we have been expecting your coming for many years!'

I baulked at this immediately, 'Many years? That is impossible! I am only twelve, and even I didn't know I was coming until a few days ago, and if I am really honest I do not even know where we are!' I took another gulp of the beetle brew and immediately wished I hadn't, wincing at the burn in my stomach.

Surprisingly, it was Quibble who answered.

'Master Joshua, you must remember that time operates in a different way here in the Kaharian from how it does on earth. The blinking of the eye in Middleofnowhereshire may be a thousand generations in the Kaharian, or vice versa.

'It is a place outside of time and as for where we are, from the springs and the caves, I am thinking this may be En Gedi.'

Heman sat back a little and nodded appreciatively at Quibble's knowledge and understanding.

'Bravo, Mr. Quibble. You are obviously well versed in the scripture and other writings of the Kaharian. You are correct on both counts of time and place.

'Given your demonstrable aptitude, I am a little surprised you are not aware of my family.'

'Alas, Lord Heman, it seems to be something of a blackspot in my learning.'

'Ah, I can discern you tell the truth, as if you had knowledge of the Sons of Korah, you would know I am quite undeserving of the title "Lord".'

Quibble looked puzzled. 'How so, sir? You are the leader of a great company of men. By definition, you are their Lord.'

'My brothers and I call only one, "Lord". You see, Mr. Quibble, Master Joshua, in the early days of the earth, our ancestor Korah was a very great man who found favour with the Great I Am, and yet when he and his followers were asked to show their loyalty, all they showed was the rebellion and pride in their hearts.

'Korah and his followers were exiled, and shame was brought on our family name. We became a clan of vagrants, outcasts and no-goods, cursing the Pidaja for abandoning us, but then, one of my kin said, "Enough! We have brought this misery upon ourselves. Do we only give praise to the I Am when good is bestowed upon us, and curse when an ill-wind sweeps in, an ill-wind we ourselves caused? I will give praise to the Great I Am all my days, whether fair or foul, and I will seek his forgiveness for the cheat and the swindler I have become."

'With that, my ancestor began to sing:

"We have heard it with our ears;
our ancestors have told us
what you did in their days,
in days long ago.
In you we make our boast all day long,
and we will praise your name forever."'

As Heman sang the words his ancestor had sung, he closed his eyes and it was as though a new spirit entered the room. I felt my head begin to spin (and it was not the beetle brew!) as I was drawn back into the enchantment of the heavenly music that had drawn us into the cave.

As the song closed, Heman opened his eyes and the spell broke gently over us.

'Since my ancestors needed to be forgiven so many wrongs, we still worship he who holds forgiveness in his palm. We were forgiven much, so we worship much.

'That, gentlemen, is why my brothers do not speak. They have dedicated their voices to I Am. Every utterance that passes their lips is in praise of him.

'Their voices are normally too lovely for human ears to endure. The man that has not music in himself, nor is moved with concord of sweet sounds, is fit for treasons, stratagems and spoils. That you can hear them and not be afraid means that you have been brought here for a reason.'

The tale had drawn tears from the bulbous eyes of Innocent Quibble, and he said, 'Yes, sir, yes, I believe we have.'

I turned to my new-found beloved, 'Cara, do you sing?'

She smiled and Heman replied, 'Cara Lily does not, but she provides inspiration through her grace of movement, she provides care and healing, as you have already witnessed. Cara Lily is the Doe of the Morning. She heralds the new day with dance!'

I sat up keenly.

'Would you dance for us?' I enquired, perhaps too boldly.

'I will dance, Joshua, but not for you. I dance only to the glory of I Am.'

She stood abruptly and disappeared from the room. Heman also stood, and beckoned us to do the same.

'Come, my friends! Join us in praise!'

We went through to another chamber, where a small group of two dozen or so men knelt in silence, their heads bowed and their arms stretched high above them.

At the front, a single musician played a lyre, golden and ornate, its song lyrical and majestic.

Although that was as naught against the vision that now fell before my eyes: my dear (or even my *deer!*) Cara bedecked in silks of ivory and gold, flowing and twisting as she walked. I saw her large eyes look up at me, and I thought I caught the trace of a smile behind the fine veil that covered the lower part of her face.

Her headdress was set with bejewelled flowers, with chains of daisies adorning her slim arms.

The lyre took up a different melody and Cara began to move her arms and body in rhythm to the music, each movement sensual and full of grace, her toes extended, her hands caressing the air. Then the assembly of brothers began to sing as she danced:

'My heart is stirred by a noble theme
as I recite my verses for the King;
my tongue is the pen of a skilful writer.
You are the most excellent of men
and your lips have been anointed with grace,
since God has blessed you forever.
Gird your sword on your side, you mighty one;
clothe yourself with splendour and majesty.
In your majesty ride forth victoriously
in the cause of truth, humility and justice.
your throne will last for ever and ever.
All your robes are fragrant with myrrh and aloes and cassia;
from palaces adorned with ivory
the music of the strings makes you glad.
All glorious is the princess within her chamber;
her gown is interwoven with gold.
Led in with joy and gladness,
they enter the palace of the King.
I will perpetuate your memory through all generations;
therefore the nations will praise you for ever and ever.'

I had not yet encountered an angel at that time (save for my grandfather, who was somewhat past his celestial prime) but Cara Lily danced with the lithe spirit and elegance of those fair creatures.

I was enraptured. The combination of music and movement stirred my soul, lifting them to an elevation of thought and feeling beyond my wildest imaginings of ecstasy; and yet in that same moment, a sense of my own "smallness" in a greater scheme, the extraordinary and the ordinary merging to give praise to the Creator, the Pidaja, the Great I Am. One whose name I had heard and yet I did not know.

At the end of the song, Cara danced her way down the aisle. I beamed at her and earnestly enthused, 'That was the most beautiful thing I have ever seen and heard.'

'Praise be! I'm glad you liked it. It was a wedding song!' With those words, she skipped off into the dark, leaving me in a state of ecstatic befuddlement.

Heman now signalled to Quibble, who followed him, head bowed slightly.

I waited in the circular room with the remaining brothers, who again fell to their knees in silent adulation as the lyre played on.

I started to take in my surroundings. The walls of the caves were coated in faint drawings. Faint because they were depicted in an ochre paint or dye against the golden rock. The paintings depicted a battle. Humans, angels, daemons, all in warfare against the other, some of the humans fighting amongst themselves, even some of the angels fighting amongst themselves, as the daemons looked on laughing. As the painting continued around the room, there was an image of a giant hand, and a group of the humans climbing onto the hand where they knelt and bowed their heads, just as the Sons of Korah bowed down now beside me.

Perhaps the hand belonged to the Pidaja. Perhaps it was possible that he did forgive the rebellion against him.

My mind began to race: perhaps, then, there is hope for my grandfather?

With that thought, I got down on my knees.

FIFTY FOUR

LUCY AND PRIMO AQUILA had passed some time in silence by the fireside.

Our grandfather's admission that 'Perhaps you are right' had rather stunned both of them. Neither was quite sure where to take the conversation after that quite out of character piece of concession.

Lucy decided to try again. 'Is there a way for you to say sorry to the Pidaja?'

She had misjudged the level of remorse Aquila had reached, as he leapt on her words, springing from his chair with an agility that was quite at odds with his frailty.

'Sorry? It is he who should apologise to me. Look what he has made me. A monster! I was once the image of light and life itself, and now I am nothing but a twisted heap of flesh. I will curse him to my last breath.

'There is no way back for me. If Joshua and Quibble return with the box...' He hesitated, but then with greater defiance affirmed, '*When* Joshua and Quibble return with the box, I will discover the secret of eternal life, I will overcome his decree, and I will destroy him and his world of men forever!'

Lucy was not shocked by the scale of the old daemon's anger, just saddened.

She said nothing.

He sneered at her. 'Nothing to say now? You pathetic little brat! You know nothing of the world or the vindictive hand of the one who controls you like puppets. He is the Pidaja, the 'keeper', because he 'keeps' you in servitude and lowliness, happy with your pointless, feeble existence. But I, who have known true greatness, have seen him for the manipulator he is!'

Lucy choked back emotion now, determined that he was not going to make her cry. 'Miss Tibbs said...'

'Do not mention that witch!'

But Lucy would not be deterred. 'Miss Tibbs said that the Pidaja keeps us in his love and grace. He is our creator and protector. I never fully understood what that meant, Grandfather, but as I see how bitter and twisted you have become by his absence in your life, I become more sure that Miss Tibbs spoke true, and I become more grateful for the love and grace that she showed me for the Pidaja's, the Great I Am's, sake.

The old man extended himself to his full height and let out an almighty, unearthly wail. He slammed his hand against a table, knocking it flying, and then he was gone.

WHEN PICARDO CAME A WHILE LATER, Lucy had restored the table to its correct place and was undertaking to collect pieces of broken porcelain from the tea-dampened rug.

She caught her finger on a sharp edge and a ball of crimson formed in her skin before forming a rivulet down her hand.

The servant came to her aid.

'Miss Lucy, please allow me.' He took the china from her hand and held his fingers tight against the blood flow.

Then, the strangest thing. He blew on the wounded digit and in an instant the cut closed itself and the stream of red dissipated to nothing.

Lucy looked at him and he looked back, not quite knowing what to say, before apologetically offering, 'Do not think me a great magician or healer, miss. It is but a parlour trick. I have not the faith for greater acts of goodness. I would that I did, as I could have saved many.'

Lucy, wise Lucy, chose this moment to challenge the elderly manservant, 'And yet you seem to have some little faith. Perhaps a glass full of faith is as sufficient as an ocean.'

'Perhaps, miss. Though for those I might have saved, whatever faith I have comes too late for them.'

'There is still one it might save, Picardo.'

'Oh, you are indeed good, Miss Lucia, but I would caution not to pin hopes on making good your grandfather. The only chance for him lies in your brother's safe return.'

'But that will not restore him to the angel he once was.'

'No, no it will not.'

Lucy changed tack now. 'You never told me what became of you after... well, after Amara... passed away.'

'There is little to tell. I became your grandfather's most trusted lieutenant, and he my most trusted master. I did his bidding. I strategised and plotted the rebellions against the Pidaja here on earth. I killed many who would have stood in the way of your grandfather and the Morning Star.'

'But why did you rebel against the Pidaja?'

'I had little idea of the game I was involved in, miss, and the dire consequences it would bring. Do remember at that time, your grandfather was an angel of the Kaharian, he was light and just and totally enthralling to be with. I was a mere soldier, and a celestial one sought my counsel! Can you imagine the thrill and the status that gave me?

'And maybe that thrill became addictive. Maybe it clouded my judgement. I had no grudge against the Pidaja when I became your grandfather's servant, and yet when Lord Aquila made me think of the suffering and the horror of the battlefield that I had seen in my years at war, when I thought of the anguish and injustice we fought to overcome, and in fighting caused more anguish, injustice, death, and destruction, where was the Pidaja then? Had he kept us from hurt? No. Had he kept us from harm? No.

'Your grandfather convinced me that the Pidaja wanted the world of men to suffer, and that the Morning Star wished to set men free.

'I know now that it was a lie.'

'Then why have you stayed loyal, so many years?'

'Because your grandfather was loyal to me, and because I was afraid of what awaited me outside of his protection.

'I did many terrible things in those days of conflict, Miss Lucy, and the justice of the rope would befall me should I venture beyond Kerioth. Men will have their vengeance.

'I have also hoped, miss, that your presence here might help rediscover the good that once dwelt in Lord Aquila. That he might turn away from the path of darkness, seek forgiveness and die in peace.'

'Do you pray, Mr. Picardo... I mean, to the Pidaja, as Miss Tibbs did when... well, before she died?'

'Yes, Miss Lucia, yes, I do. I pray for absolution.'

FIFTY FIVE

THIS NEXT INSTALLMENT in my chronicle, I must confess, came to be second hand from Mr. Quibble. The veracity of its contents I cannot vouch for, but to this point in the narrative he had been a trustworthy source of information.

At the conclusion of Cara's marvellous dance, as I have previously mentioned, Heman summoned Innocent Quibble, my travelling companion, into another cave (there really was quite a complex of the things inside that hillside!)

There they were seated in a darkened room, lit only by candles. Heman poured another goblet of the beetle brew at which Quibble smiled graciously, although he tried not to think of its ingredients as he took a polite little sip.

Heman proceeded to pick up an eight stringed instrument, which he gently plucked at almost absent-mindedly as he opened what apparently was an informal conversation.

'We are most glad to have you with us, Mr. Quibble, and I give thanks that you found us again.'

Quibble swallowed back the mouthful of drink that he was in the midst of and burbled, 'Yes, quite.'

'We have not chanced upon many fellow humans in recent times. So your being here brings us much joy. Having been an exiled people on earth, we greatly appreciate the fellowship that is occasionally, by his grace, afforded us here.

'Tell me; what brings you here?'

Quibble snapped out of the relaxed bonhomie he had been enjoying, and the solicitor in him started to sense a trap in the questioning. He looked deep and hard into Heman's flinty eyes.

'You know full well why we are here, sir. By your own confession, you have expected us these many years. I am no fool.'

Heman smiled acknowledging that his guest was alert to his methods. 'Ah, yes, there you are right, Mr. Quibble. I have indeed been foretold of your coming and I am aware of your goal, or at least that of the one who sent you.

'I must confess, I am unclear of the Great I Am's purposes in allowing you to progress with this surely deadly quest, but it is not for me to try to fathom, simply to trust.

'But, sir, you misunderstand me; my question is what are *you* doing here? You, Innocent Quibble. What made you part of the heinous scheme of an overreaching traitor?'

Quibble bridled slightly at the question but something within him made him want to open up.

'Ah, sir, I could bristle at your rather blunt assessment of the man I call my master and yet I know it in my heart to be true.

'Why I, you ask? Why Innocent Quibble and not some other lackey in thrall of the great mind-tricks of a devious old daemon? I have asked myself that same question, and through this insane quest, the devastating consequences of which I am fully aware, should it prove successful, I have wondered why he chose me above any other.

'I am not built for agility or speed; I could not steal in like a thief in the night. I have knowledge but lack application of that knowledge at times. I am not brave; in fact, my courage has come mainly from the perseverance of a twelve-year-old boy. I do not know if we can succeed in this venture, and there is a part of me unsure that I even want to succeed.

'So, in short, I do not know why it is I who is here and not some other.'

Heman searched Quibble deeply and silently with his eyes for some moments. 'And still, Primo Aquila – and I will use his name for it holds no power here – asked you, and you have been able to progress so far in this journey in spite of many obstacles.

'I think you underestimate yourself, Mr. Quibble. You have told me all the qualities you do not possess, but nothing of those that you do possess. It is those things that have allowed you to be here.

'I want you to think of the barriers you have faced and, at each, you have overcome through a quality you have shown. You have been brought here because there is something you must do before you can leave.

'You are not my prisoner, Mr. Quibble. You are free to go, but you will not get far if you do not learn the lesson of this part of your journey.

'You will remember that I told you that we worship day and night with all our hearts and souls, because we were forgiven a great many wrongs. That is what this place is. It is where people come in search of forgiveness.

'You would not have had the ears to hear our song, unless our song was for you.'

Quibble just looked at him, before bursting into uncontrollable sobs.

Quite what he confessed to or sought forgiveness for that night, he never disclosed to me, but I do know when next I saw him he seemed lighter in his expression.

For myself, as I knelt in that chamber with my arms lifted to the sky, I simply said sorry that I had not loved my grandfather as I wished I had, and I felt whatever anger I had inside me lifted. It felt good.

I opened my eyes as Heman and Quibble returned to the room.

'You are ready to leave.' I heard the gentle trot of dainty hooves and a moist, warm nose nuzzle against my arm. 'Cara will be your guide.'

THE SONS OF KORAH ROBED US in taupe coloured tunics, like their own, and I was grateful to be wearing two sturdy sandals instead of just one unsuitable leather shoe.

There was no time for long goodbyes as Cara, now in the form of the Doe of the Morning, started to make her way down the tunnel and out into the dawn's first light.

As we left, Heman nodded his head to bid us adieu and simply said, 'It is better to take refuge in the Lord than to trust in man.'

At that early stage of my blossoming feelings for Cara, it did not strike me as at all odd that the girl whom I loved occasionally walked around in the shape of a deer. Perhaps what they say about love being blind is true. To my young eyes she was perfection.

Cara set a brisk pace and we sometimes had to break into a light jog to keep up. Quibble held his side lightly, suffering from stitch, but his countenance remained bright, as though there had been a subtle but significant change within him.

We journeyed in silence until the deer turned to us and spoke, 'We are approaching the abandoned fortress. You must be warned that you will see and hear things that may seem odd to you; things that may disturb you.'

I thought I'd try a little humour. 'Like a talking deer, for instance.'

The short, soft fur around her eyes wrinkled slightly, and her round dewy eyes narrowed. 'This isn't something to be laughed at, Joshua. Many have entered this place and never been seen again.'

I lowered my eyes feeling slightly ashamed and hoping she did not think me a fool.

Quibble looked more concerned with what lay ahead. 'This is Babel. We must hold onto our wits, lest we surrender our sanity.'

I too now looked to the silhouetted ruined buildings that lay ahead. 'What is in there?'

'Only what we take with us, Joshua,' he replied. 'Our deepest fears, our hidden desires, our pasts and our futures, our insecurities and our vanity. It has driven many a good man mad. We must be on our guard.'

With trepidation we continued on and the fortress grew larger before us. At its centre was a tower; although ruined and decaying, it loomed large above us in the pink-hued early morning sky.

I breathed heavily, trying to control the anxiety I felt. Cara spoke to try to ease the tension.

'I will be walking ahead of you both all the way. Whatever happens, just keep walking and fix your eyes on me.'

THE DESERTED FORTRESS was a place of terror for me. Just a handful of months ago, by my perception, Lucy and I had come across a place such as this; a rugged, ruined castle set high on a hill. We had spent hours running the rule over every inch of its spiralling stairways, battle scarred turrets and unbreachable defences that, judging by its decaying state, had presumably at one time been breached.

That place breathed with the memories of battles won and lost, of lives given and taken in protection of some cause; a proud history, a noble history.

We had imagined ourselves as troops defending the keep; two gallant soldiers protecting our right to a life free from oppression, as we imagined so many had over the centuries.

Yet now, as I stepped into Babel, it did not breathe life into thoughts of noble quests. No, it rather sucked the very life from you. The air was thick with some insidious lust for something; something dangerous. It had the reek of vain ambition gone bad.

The central tower now lurked over us casting a monolithic shadow on the central square. How such a feat of engineering had been accomplished I had no concept, and while it may have been a masterpiece of imagination and creation, judging by the featureless, cold, empty square beneath it, it had brought only death and destruction.

A light wind swept across the dustbowl, occasionally lifting up clouds of sandy soil. It was a welcome distraction from the bland monotony of the surroundings.

I tried to keep my eyes fixed on the deer-girl Cara, just ahead of me, and the sight of her was always a welcome one, but the dust clouds were becoming more and more of a distraction and now I found myself taken by the sight of them. For now, as much as I told myself otherwise, I was convinced that they were forming shapes.

I moved my eyes away from Cara and then I was gone.

It happened like a punch to the stomach as all the air was taken from me by a squall. The sound at first was like a deafening last whirl of bath water disappearing down the plug hole.

My head began to pound, my vision inconstant, colourless, clouded.

I found myself being drawn toward the cloud shapes, but what did I see? What did I see?

A MAN; YES! A MAN AND A WOMAN. Adults. Perhaps in their twenties and they are each holding something; something small; something precious as they hold it tight in both arms. They look down longingly at the packages. No, not packages. Children. Two children. It is my parents! They are holding Lucy and me! They speak. I cannot hear them. I move closer. They speak again. Both together now, but not the same words. And then another voice. Stronger, darker, deeper. It whispers in a rasping, guttural growl and a tongue I do not recognise. Then another voice. Each on top of the other. Rising. Rising. Layer on layer of sound. A kaleidoscope of sound. Always moving, never fixed. Constantly drawing focus and then turning away.

The cloud of dust evaporates, my parents shouting into my uncomprehending ears.

Another image. The baby Lucy is left lying on the floor. She grows. She grows rapidly, turning into a toddler, turning into a young girl, turning into a woman, young, then middle aged, then elderly. Turning and twisting. She is in pain. I move toward her. She screams, her cries piercing to my ears as the rasping, dark voice incants something over her. Her body straightens; every muscle tort. Her back now arches in agony before going limp and lifeless. The only sound is silence before the cloud explodes into another scene.

Flowers fall from the sky. Sepia tones. I am there. I am fully grown. Smartly dressed, my hair neatly brushed. I am smiling. The imagined me turns to my left and there is Cara, more beautiful than ever, wrapped in an ivory silk gown. She holds flowers. Her hair is plaited with jewels. My heart is light. I slip a thin band of gold onto her delicate finger and... and we kiss! The kiss lingers as trumpets sound, but then, as we kiss, our faces start to wrinkle and age. I look at my hands as they start to decay and crumble. I am dying. The trumpets turn into a cacophony of screeching strings, dissonant and fearful. I am dying.

As the image starts to disperse I suddenly find myself (the real me) hitting the ground. I come to with the feeling of a doe's rough tongue on my fair, boyish cheek.

INNOCENT QUIBBLE PICKED HIMSELF UP and dusted sand from his new garb, which only seemed to accentuate his roundness.

'What happened?' I mumbled; my head slightly fuzzy as I got to my feet.

'I had to rugby tackle you, young man.'

Cara continued, 'You were having hallucinations, Joshua. Mr. Quibble broke the hold of the enchantment over you.'

'I am grateful. Thank you.'

'Please, dear boy, don't mention it.'

I rubbed my eyes as I readjusted to reality. 'What was that?'

'This place means "Confusion". A person's mind can be twisted and distorted until they become quite mad, following the dust clouds to the top of the tower and plummeting to their deaths. They hear multitudes of voices and see things that break them and make them consumed with desire and lose the people they truly are.'

'Are the visions real?'

'Some are. Others are deep fears or deep desires.'

'Some of the things I saw... scared me. Can I stop those things from happening?'

Quibble and Cara looked at each other hesitantly, and the solicitor spoke, 'I do not know, Joshua. I do not know.'

Cara looked around. 'We should hurry from this place. Joshua, climb upon my back – I can see I will need to keep a keen eye on you!'

The deer winked one of her long-lashed eyes at me, and we were on our way again.

FIFTY SIX

'ABSOLUTION?' LUCY ASKED, slightly uncertain what the word meant.

'Forgiveness for my wrongdoings; of which there have been many.' The old manservant swallowed hard now. 'I have been a terrible man, miss, and perhaps my continued service to Lord Aquila is at odds with my deep regret, but your grandfather is not only my master of these many years, miss. I love him as though he were my brother. To see his decay and desolation as he faces death breaks my heart. I will be by his side until the end.'

'But you love the Pidaja, too?'

'As I have reflected on my life, miss, as I have wandered this castle, mainly alone for many years while your grandfather was elsewhere, the hope of being restored to him has been my greatest joy. I stay as I would have Lord Aquila know that joy again also.'

'Tell me about the Pidaja, Mr. Picardo, please. Miss Tibbs spoke of him, but it seemed like fairy stories to our young ears.'

'It is no fairy story. He is real; majestic and glorious. The creator of all things; from the vast lake beyond these walls to every cute freckle on your nose. He made them all and he loves them all.'

'I should like to meet him one day!' Lucy enthused.

'If you say that to yourself each morning, miss, and live your day with that on your heart, then one day you will.'

Joy resided in Lucy's heart, but then her mind turned.

'Mr. Picardo, if Josh succeeds and my grandfather does gain everlasting life, what will happen?'

The old man's face slackened and the twinkle that had been present in his eye until this point in the conversation was suddenly extinguished.

'Oh miss, your grandfather means to challenge the Pidaja, the Great I Am, for the throne. If your grandfather learns the secret of eternal life, he will have overcome the word of the I Am, and will use that to rail the enemies of the Kaharian to challenge I Am's authority. It will be the war to end all wars. Oh my, miss, I have been a fool to help facilitate the daemon's wicked scheme. No good can come of this. He has only lust for power in his heart. He is a monster! And I, the monster's fool!'

No sooner had the words left Picardo's lips than the door flew upon and Primo Aquila was upon the servant; his long, gnarled right hand grabbing Picardo by his thin neck.

'A monster, am I? Then know, my "old friend", just how monstrous I can be!'

He raised his left hand high above his head as Picardo looked up in horror to see the cold, shining blade that Aquila gripped.

Lucy pulled at our grandfather's leg, screaming at him, imploring him to stop, but in the giddy euphoria of hate that pulsed through the daemon's veins, her piercing cries never reached his ear as he brought down the knife between Picardo's shoulders, his frail skin and bone yielding easily to its point.

The servant's knees crumbled and his jerking body slumped to the floor, breathing heavily as he gasped for whatever air he could.

But Primo Aquila was not finished. He had the blade still in his hand, holding it triumphantly above him as crimson blood dripped from it. His eyes were wide and bright, his tongue lolling over his bottom lip, like a beast.

With a brutal force he threw the knife into the fireplace where it burst into an explosion of purple light, and the fire raged.

Picardo tried to cry out, 'Repent, my Lord!' but it was no use.

'Shekanak abolath mech tremalon shebakath!' the daemon chanted over the writhing body of his old manservant, each word bringing fresh pain to his wretched body.

Lucy backed, terrified, into the corner as the torture unfolded before her.

'Nekanaka quilatamo shebakath ech tamalata! Ne bes sheknak bei porira nem!'

Aquila dropped to one knee beside the twisting, tortured body of Picardo, his right hand held, suspended inches away from the old retainer's face as he continued his curse. 'A monster I am indeed! And I am your master! Say I am your only master, and all will be forgiven. Say, "You, Primo Aquila, are my only master!"'

Picardo was silent, and Aquila chanted the curse again, causing Picardo to writhe, screaming in agony. Grandfather yelled at his old friend: 'Say it! Say it now! I am your master!'

Suddenly, Picardo's face, distorted by tears and pain, relaxed and became calm, his eyes opened wide.

'I have but one master...'

Aquila grinned at his apparent triumph, but Picardo continued.

'...and he is the high King, the creator of all, the Great I Am.'

My grandfather's face fell and he swallowed hard. He looked deep into his old servant's eyes before whispering, 'So be it!'

With that he lowered his hand over Picardo's face and sharply twisted his neck.

Then all was still.

PART FIVE

Judgement

Fifty Seven

WE LEFT BABEL IN QUICK TIME, with me still draped over Cara's back, Quibble trotting alongside us on his dumpy legs.

Through the grand gates we found ourselves in what I can only describe as a lush green garden.

It appeared to be wild – trees, grasses and flowers growing freely – and at the same time it felt as though it was tended with the utmost detail and love.

As we entered, Cara uttered a strange little statement. She simply said, 'Do not talk to the animals!' which was odd in itself, but even odder coming from the lips of a talking deer!

After a period of rest, I felt strong enough to walk on my own legs again and so the three of us made our way through the beautiful garden.

As desolate as Babel had been, so this place abounded with life. At every turn there was the chirp of a bird, the scuttle of an insect, the rustle of something small and furry in the undergrowth. It felt as though all life was cradled there.

Quibble and I walked together behind Cara, and as we walked I noticed that the solicitor was silently crying.

'Is something troubling you, Mr. Quibble?' I enquired as sensitively as a twelve-year-old knows how.

He dabbed his eye with the back of his hand. 'Ah, it is nothing, dear boy. It is only... it is only I wish so very much that I could walk in this place with my boy; my son. I have been so very cruel to him in his short life. We have never been for a walk. Not in daylight, anyway. I felt it best to shield him from the unkind stares and comments of others. What I would give to go back and take his hand and walk together through the forest, or run barefoot in the long grass on warm summer days. I only hope I can be forgiven for my folly.

'There are so many things I have got wrong. All those people I lied to, that I wilfully misled in my false teaching after I met Lucian. My longsuffering wife, a truly good woman, who was made an outcast by my treacherous doings; and that poor boy who I have never once told how much I love him.'

'Then let us hope we can get this thing done and soon be returned to them,' I said, laying my hand on his arm.

'Joshua, it is not solely their forgiveness I must seek...'

We continued in silence, beating a winding path through that calm, pastoral idyll. I knew not where we were going but I trusted our guide with my life.

I felt a complete peace as I walked there; although creatures appeared unannounced at regular intervals, some of them quite fierce in appearance, it did not trouble any of us. It was a place of safety, and more than once on that long trail I wondered why anyone would ever want to leave here... and yet besides Quibble, Cara (though not in her present four-legged form) and me, there were no other people. It was the perfect place to live. Springs flowed with water, the air was warm and clear, the trees provided shelter and an abundance of life and food. Why were there no people?

I left the question in my head, perhaps not wanting to know the answer at this stage. There were still things that, as a twelve-year-old, I was not quite ready to understand.

The light dwindled in the sky and Cara took us away from our apparent track into a small copse. Quibble opened some provisions and we ate wearily without speaking. In no time, Quibble was on his back, snoring loudly. Butterflies came and fluttered in the air around him, dancing in the stream of his noisy exhalations.

Cara and I laughed as we watched. She was now in her human form (she said it was easier to walk as a deer, but eat as a human).

I looked at her intently as her wide smile glistened in the fading light.

'Cara? The mission Mr. Quibble and I are on... is it very dangerous?'

The smile dimmed a little and she looked at me earnestly, 'Josh. It is the most insanely dangerous thing I have ever heard of. I don't even believe it is a good thing, and still, I think it is something you have to do.'

That reality hung heavily in the air between us before she continued, 'Besides, I will be there for you every step of the journey, if you would like me to be.'

I gulped hard while bumbling, 'Yes, I'd like that a lot.' Only I wasn't that eloquent and it came out more as, 'Yesssidlikethatalot.'

Thankfully, she carried on talking in that gentle, tender, lilting voice, although what she said next was rather odd: 'I am so glad to have finally met you after years of hearing about you!'

I don't recall actually saying anything in response, but I can only imagine that my expression involved the raising of my eyebrows right up to my hairline.

'Oh, I can see I have confused you. You see, we have a friend in common; one of my oldest and dearest friends. You know her as Angela Agnes Tibbs.'

At this stage my eyebrows probably went as far as the crown of my head! Cara Lily giggled her charming giggle.

'Oh dear, oh, you really had no idea, did you? Miss Tibbs was no ordinary governess. She was your guardian angel.

'When your grandfather fell, the angels of the Kaharian were keen to ensure that you and your sister did not fall immediately into the devilish clutches of your grandfather. So, a muse was sent to be your protector. She made herself mortal to take care of you, but in the sure and certain knowledge of the love of the Great I Am, and his protection over her life.

'She told me all about you. She loves you and Lucy very much. She still looks over you now, since she has herself returned to the Kaharian. I didn't want her to do it because I would miss her presence, and I definitely didn't want her to call herself 'Angela' – I thought that was a dead giveaway!'

'I had no idea,' I stuttered. 'You say she was a muse? Is that what you are?'

'Yes, Miss Tibbs inspired works of great art, and I inspire beautiful music. I am called the Doe of the Morning.'

I sat back as I tried to take this all in.

'Cara, when we were in Babel I saw things. I saw things involving you... you and me, both of us, together. It was...' I blushed now as I spoke. 'It was...nice!'

'Nice?'

'We seemed happy together. Was that vision real? I mean could you and I...?'

Before I could say more, she put one finger against my lips to halt me, the porcelain tip of her digit pressed lovingly against my plump pink lips.

'Josh, what you saw was the desire of your heart. Because you saw it, does not make it so, and if you set your heart too firmly toward that goal it will only lead to pain. However, if it is the will of he who made us both, in our similarities and our differences, then it will be as you saw.'

I leant toward her, I could feel her warm breath on my cheeks. I closed my eyes and moved closer. Our lips touched, gently at first and then more firmly as she stroked my face with her hand. I opened my eyes to see her looking deep within me, her eyes dancing with light and... love!

FIFTY EIGHT

AS THE SUN ROSE IN THE SKY, we were already on our way.

How long that kiss had lasted, I do not know, but after a few awkward but tender giggles and sideways glances, it was time to awaken Quibble from his noisy slumber and set off.

Cara Lily, my love, my muse, my angel, was returned to being the Doe of the Morning, and strode elegantly, confidently, ahead of us.

Did I imagine it, or was there an extra lightness in her step that morning? (I probably did imagine it!)

In contrast to the bounding excitement that made my heart leap, Quibble seemed quite perturbed and restless, and was frequently darting his glance left and right as we made our way.

'Is everything quite alright, Mr. Quibble?'

'I am sure it is me being a dolt, young sir, but I cannot seem to shake a sense that we are being followed.'

My eyes shot to the dense grass to our left where I picked out, only pinpricks from a distance but distinct against the dark backdrop, two glimmering ovals of green light.

The same ovals of green light that I had seen at Allon Bakuth, the Oak of Weeping: the pantera!

I yelled, 'Quickly, run, it's a pantera!' but I immediately found myself flat on my back as I collided unceremoniously with the unmoving rear quarters of my dearest deer, who was just laughing as the creature emerged from his hiding place.

Quibble was rooted to the spot and turned on Cara, 'What devilry is this? Have you lured us here to laugh as we are savaged by this beast?'

Cara laughed again. Had I been deceived? Was this a trap?

'Oh, my friends! Do you not see? Can you not see who it is? It is Astrador!'

I am sure by this stage in the narrative, it is to be wondered at that I had any eyebrows left at all as they again lifted in bewilderment at this revelation.

I lay prone on the floor as the enormous creature, silky black fur glimmering in the early morning light, muscles rippling with power, loomed over me and then nuzzled my arm. I responded in trepidation, extending my hand and rubbing the top of the beast's head. I held my breath, which was good, because it allowed me to hear a contented purr come from deep in the pantera's throat.

I looked into those quizzical feline eyes and asked, 'Asti? Is that really you?' The big cat just curled up next to me, lolling his head happily onto my chest, just as though we were back in Tibbs' cottage sitting by the fire as we toasted marshmallows.

'I cannot believe it!' I exclaimed, not knowing what else to say.

'Oh, there is so much you have to learn and believe, Josh. In the Kaharian, all is not as it seems to your earthly eyes, but it is exactly as it was made to be.

'Yes, Astrador is a pantera who took the form of a domestic cat when he was with Tibethia, that is, your Miss Tibbs.'

Quibble blustered, dumbfounded, 'But he tried to kill us! At the Oak, he ran at us and tried to rip us limb from limb!'

'He just wanted to play! He came to the Kaharian to help you.'

'Oh...' seemed the only response either of us could muster.

So we continued, the deer, the cat, the toad and the boy, until the woodland seemed to thin out, and a small brick path became visible beneath our feet.

As I clearly knew so little about the ways of the Kaharian, and understood even less, I thought it best to ask a question rather than make any assumptions.

'Where does this path lead us?'

Cara looked over her shoulder. 'To where we want to go!' she answered enigmatically, and the truth at that moment was the only place I really wanted to go was home, but she continued, 'It leads to the citadel. The palace of the King of all. The Great I Am.'

FIFTY NINE

THE FIRE STILL BURNED PURPLE in the silent drawing room. In one corner, my sister Lucy sat crumpled, eyes reddened, choking back tears, hardly breathing from the terror she had just witnessed.

In another corner, just a few feet away, but so detached that he could have been on another planet, sat Primo Aquila, eyes reddened, blazing with barely contained fury, skin dripping with cold sweat.

Between them lay the still warm body of Antonius Picardo, his form lifeless, but his face an image of calm tranquillity.

Before their eyes, the body started to rapidly crumble, flesh and bone dissolving into dust. The dust then lifted into the air, and with an almost soundless puff, was gone. There was no trace of the life that had just been snuffed out.

The fire started to die out, and Lucy spoke, though not moving her eyes from the spot where the body had lain.

'Grandfather, what have you done? What have you done?'

'Shut up, you bleating little idiot, unless you wish the same fate to befall you.

'He was a traitor to me. All I gave him, and he turned his back at the time I would need him most. When the chance of my return to my rightful place was at hand; when all we once fought for would be restored. He betrayed me.'

'He did not betray you. He loved you as his brother.'

'I have no brother, no equal upon this wretched earth. My place is on the throne of power, and all will bow to me and call me Lord!'

Lucy unfurled herself from the tightly curled ball she sat in, and lifted her head high with dignity as she made her way unsteadily to the door. As she opened it to leave, she looked down on the daemon who sat nearby, a mix of fear and pity in her eyes.

'I love you, Grandfather, and I will stay with you, but I will never call you Lord.'

SIXTY

THE PATH WAS PLAIN AND WEATHERED. The roughly interlocking bricks were off-white in colour and uneven under our feet. I did not take my eyes from the path for several hours (by my reckoning) until they came to an abrupt halt and I cast my eyes upwards.

There before me, resplendent, was a white city on a hillside; its walls and conical turrets and towers were pristine and elegant. Pennants and flags fluttered in a gentle breeze, and music filled the air, even though we were still some distance from a single, colossal gate that seemed to be the only way in or out.

We made our silent progress up the steep slope that led to the golden entrance. Along the walls of the city, a long line of winged, white statues stood as sentinels... except, as I drew closer, I realised that they were not statues at all... they were angels! Dozens of angels, each beautifully cloaked in light.

A thought suddenly struck me, and I voiced it to the angelic one who led us up the path now. 'We seem to have many eyes on us, Cara. How are we going to get in?'

'There is only one way into the citadel, and that is through the door.'

I breathed deeply. Her answer had not filled me with great confidence. 'And how will we get through the door?'

'We will knock.'

I have grown used to Cara's logical, straightforward answers in the intervening years, in fact she was a lot like Lucy in that respect, but at that moment in time it frustrated me and I responded in the way a twelve-year-old might (bearing in mind, I was a twelve-year-old at this juncture).

'Look, I am sorry, but that really isn't very comforting. If I am to do this thing I have been bidden to do, and I still don't really know why I am doing it, I want to know I am going to be coming out of this alive and going home to my sister. Frankly, you giving matter-of-fact answers about things that might cost me my life really isn't helping much. If those angels are going to hurl down fire and brimstone on my head the moment I walk in there, I would like to know about it, and then you can show me the path home.'

I immediately blushed, knowing I had let my emotions get the better of me. But why was I even here? For my grandfather's sake? I hardly knew him, and cared for him less still. Why should I risk my life to save his?

Cara looked hard at me with her doe eyes. Quibble and Astrador just looked to the floor. Cara then turned back into a girl and walked toward me. She stroked my cheek with her fair hand, and pressed her lips lightly against mine. I tasted a salt tear that had trickled down her face, and she moved her head backwards, wiping the tear away, and stared deep into my eyes with a look that took my breath.

'Josh, I cannot guarantee your safety. I cannot know the Great I Am's purpose in letting your grandfather progress even this far with his horrible scheme. I cannot vouch for what is on the other side of that gate, and I cannot promise I will ever see you again. All I know is that you have to do this, and even if I cannot go with you, my heart does.'

I looked at my toes as there didn't seem to be anything to say, or nothing that my childish heart could bear to say anyway. Cara led me by the hand a few steps, kissed me again and whispered in my ear, 'Knock on the door.'

Quibble came alongside me; I took a deep breath, and knocked upon a small wooden door to the side of the gilded gates.

An age seemed to pass before we heard the clunking of chains and the clicking of locks.

The door opened, and all we saw was... a foot! A giant foot! We recoiled in surprise, and then saw a giant head scoop down and look through the tiny portal.

'Aha, I wondered when I might see you!' His voice and his visage seemed strangely familiar. 'You had better come in, though just the two of you, not the shape shifters at the moment.'

I looked back to Cara, who was already transformed back to the Doe of the Morning, and she lifted her head, urging me to go in.

I turned to face front and made my way through the door.

The room was a jumble of bric-a-brac and clutter; papers and documents scattered over every surface.

The giant loomed above us, maybe twenty feet tall. 'I have been expecting you.' His accent was clipped and precise, quite at odds with his slightly shabby appearance. There was a shirt, tie and waistcoat in evidence, but they were ill-fitting and the shirt had what looked like soup stains down the front.

Yet the face was familiar.

'Have we met before?' I enquired.

'Ah no, young fellow, but my brother has spoken of you a long time since.'

'Your brother?' said the solicitor now, the first he had spoken in hours. 'I am sorry, sir, I do not recall having met a giant on our journey.'

The giant laughed a thunderous laugh. 'Why yes, my twin brother, Hadraniel Derwood!'

Quibble and I looked at one another, and Quibble continued, 'Forgive me, but you are not particularly alike in... well, size...' He gave a nervous little cough, which only led to more riotous laughter from the large one.

'Well, Mr. Quibble, as I assume you to be? When Hadraniel and I were born, we were quite identical, but as children he lived on tea and nervous energy, rushing here, there and everywhere with his wiggly little walk. I, on the other hand, was more interested in poring over the chronicles and eating great wedges of cake!' He patted his huge, rotund belly before gesturing to the scatter of papers around the room.

'I am Araunah, and delighted to make your acquaintance.' He offered a ginormous hand to each of us, and we took it in turn to clasp a single one of his huge fingers in greeting.

'Now, please do sit down. I happen to have a rather fine carrot cake with cream cheese icing on the go, if you would care for a slice? I always see carrot cake as my concession to healthy eating, my dear little men!' he chuckled as he carved off two huge slabs of delicious looking moist cake for my travelling companion and me.

We nibbled at the cake appreciatively. It was indeed exceptional, but it was also vast. I could quite see how Mr. Derwood, the larger, had grown so much on such portions.

Quibble spoke next, having swallowed down a large forkful of the exquisite cake, the frosting coating his upper lip like a pencil-thin white moustache.

'Mr. Derwood. We have passed much time in getting here; I wonder if you might be so kind as to point us in the right direction, as I assume you know why we are here.'

Araunah twiddled his fork on his already empty plate as he considered his response.

'Ah, Mr. Quibble, a man who likes to cut to the chase. I appreciate that. I can allow you access, but the real question is whether you are ready to face the prospect that you may not come out again? I know this weighs heavily on Master Joshua, but on you too, Mr. Quibble. You do know, I suppose, that should you enter this place, you may never see your wife or your son again. Is that a price you are willing to pay? Is that a sacrifice you wish to make? You need not answer, sir. I Am knows your heart, whatever may pass from your lips. You may leave by the way you came in.'

It was brutal and matter-of-fact as could be. Quibble looked shame-faced as he headed for the door. As he went, he didn't meet my eye, but put a hand on my shoulder and said, 'I wish you the very best, Joshua. It has been an honour, and I am sorry I have failed you at this final hurdle. If you make it back...' He checked himself. '*When* you make it back, I will be waiting here at the gate for you.'

And then he was gone.

The room was still as Araunah surveyed me. I continued to look at the floor.

'Mr. Derwood,' I said, voice trembling, 'I don't know what I am doing here. I am so ill-equipped for this task. I don't even like my grandfather. I miss my sister. Maybe I should just go too.'

Araunah smiled warmly back across the giant table and caught my eye.

'Young Master Joshua. You screwed your courage to the sticking post when you walked through fire and water to get here. You knew then that you may not return, and yet you made that sacrifice. The Great I Am has a purpose for you. I am not privy to what that might be, but you have got this far, through many tests and trials, by being you, being the you that he created you to be. Whatever your grandfather may plot, I Am can turn it back to good. I could tell you to have courage, young one, as I send you on your way, but you already have it, so I simply bid you to trust the path set before you, leave the past behind you and the future ahead of you. Live in this moment and be you.'

Without him moving, a door opened on the other side of the room, bright sunlight beyond it, and the sound of song. I pushed back my chair and without looking toward the giant, I walked straight ahead.

There was a small square with a spring running through it; I think I heard someone call it Gidron. There were people smiling, children playing in the crystal water, and everyone had a song on their lips. I seemed to pass them unnoticed, although I was dressed very differently to their finely tailored, colourful garments.

I looked around me in each direction, not really knowing which way to go, and then my gaze moved upwards and I instinctively knew that was where I must travel.

On one side of the square there was a flight of white marble steps, and with hurried pace I made my way over, checking no-one had followed, and started my ascent.

Sixty One

THE DAYS BROKE EARLY AT KERIOTH as spring began to turn into summer.

It had been three days since Lucy had seen Primo Aquila. He had vanished from sight after his brutal murder of Picardo. Or at least it had seemed so to Lucy, as she had locked herself in her room, alone, without food or company. In any case, the fallen angel had made no attempt to see her. Maybe it was better that way.

It was with no little trepidation that Lucy unlocked the bedroom door and made her way down the creaking steps of the magnificent central staircase.

The great house was dark and soundless as she poked her head from one room to the next. The air was musty and all the windows shuttered as though the building was preparing for a tempest whipping across the lake.

Lucy made her way into the kitchen, where once she would have found Picardo industriously rustling up a batch of scones or fresh bread, but today there was nothing. Lucy discovered a doughnut on the counter, but found it to be crusty and inedible having been left out for days.

She flung the kitchen door open and was met with a blast of bright sunlight reflecting off of the vast, glassy lake beyond the headland.

Silhouetted there against the already burning morning sun was a lone figure, black against the bright light; his frame stooped by age and upon his back two sizable protrusions, the remnants of his true identity.

He was turned in profile and Lucy could see that he clutched tightly at the walking stick that was perhaps all that kept him upright.

She tiptoed her way along the uneven path that had formed from the regular fall of her delicate feet along that route over the past several weeks.

Primo Aquila looked up as she sidled toward him, genuine surprise on his weathered old face.

'I did not expect to see you. I rather thought we had said all that was to be said between us.'

'As much as I hate what you have become, Grandfather, I do still love you for what you were and what you might be.'

His tone was sharp as he came back at her: 'Do not speak that way, you silly girl. There is no love for me. You have nothing to offer me that I could want.'

Lucy breathed deeply, trying to keep her dignity in spite of his hurtful remarks.

'If I am of no further use to you, then I will leave this place. Whatever evil you have planned, I want no part of it.'

She turned her back and headed back down the path, first walking with poise before breaking into a tearful run for the house.

'I do not want to die alone!' Aquila shouted after her, but she did not hear him. 'I am scared!' he admitted to himself.

For so long he had been fear itself, and now as the time ebbed away, he was afraid.

Sixty Two·

THE STEPS WERE SPARSELY POPULATED, but everyone seemed to be smiling, laughing, singing. A few nodded to acknowledge me (so, I was not invisible) and seemingly were not put off by my odd clothing which seemed so out of place among the fine fabrics and vibrant colours of the garb worn by the townsfolk.

The stairway wound around walls and buildings; there were little nooks and passageways in every direction but all the while I had a sense to keep going upwards, although along the narrow streets, I could not gain much of a vista as to what might be at the top of this extraordinary, beautiful city.

Every now and then, I had to stop to catch my breath. My calves burned from the climbing. How far had I come? A hundred steps, two hundred? I had not counted.

As the journey progressed, the streets became narrower, the steps became deeper, which of course meant that the hill was becoming steeper.

Each step I trod, my body seemed to hurt more, but I knew I had to keep going; another step and another. Always the same, but I had to endure it.

The crowds seemed to thin out, but then became denser again as I came closer to what I perceived as a market place. Perhaps this was where my prize lay? Would I have to buy this box? I had no money. In fact I had never even seen any money in this land or my own. Tibbs, or Tibethia as I now knew her to be, took care of everything for us.

I reached the top step and tried to peer over the heads or between the legs of the large throng that had gathered.

Indeed it did seem to be a market place... except there was no market. No stalls, no traders. Just groups of people gathered together joyfully exchanging handshakes and hugs and kisses. Was this the commerce and currency of the citadel?

The songs people sang were all different in their composition, their language, and yet the notes hung on the air like wisps of golden thread, their melodies intertwining in a glorious counterpoint that blanketed the sky with a joyous chorus. And there, over the heads of this delirious assembly, I saw it, standing proud in the centre of the square, overlooking all.

A lighthouse.

THE LIGHTHOUSE WAS NOT ESPECIALLY TALL, certainly not like the tower at Babel, nor was it particularly finely carved or intricate in its detail, but it was of the most brilliant white stone... or what I took to be stone from a distance.

I weaved my way through the crowd. Every little while I would bump into someone and rather than scowl at me, they would take me firmly by the shoulders and smile gleefully at the sight of me. It was delightfully disconcerting or disconcertingly delightful; I am not sure which, if either.

Nobody seemed to want to stop me on my progress toward this centre point of the city. For all the fortifications of the outer walls and the dozens of angels who acted as watchmen over the world outside the city, the lighthouse seemed to be completely unguarded.

I drew close. Even in the daylight, the light at the top was startling, burning incandescent blue. The brilliant white walls were almost in touching distance now, and yet I could not touch them. They were not walls of stone or brick, but of cloud.

Shimmering, ever moving spirals of cloud formed into a perfect cone.

There were no solid walls, nothing solid or permanent at all. I felt with every inch of my being that what I sought was at the top of that lighthouse, but how could I possibly get there?

I closed my eyes, resigned to the fact that my journey may end here. And then, oh, of course! 'Nothing is as it seems.' I did the only thing I could do – I stepped into the cloud.

Instantly I was swept from my feet, and yet I felt no fear. I crossed my arms across my chest, breathed deeply and closed my eyes.

Moments passed, maybe longer, and I opened my eyes again as I felt solid ground beneath my feet.

The ground was in fact the wooden floorboards of a room. A perfect circle. At the centre of the room was a small, round table, upon which sat a pocket-sized, beautifully carved oak casket inlaid with silver, and on the far side of the room, his back turned, looking out over the citadel, was a man.

He was robed in a simple white gown, his dark, wavy hair flowing past the collar.

I looked at him, unmoving for maybe minutes, and then I started to cry.

SIXTY THREE

MY CHEEKS BECAME DASHED with streams of salt water, and the man must have heard my blubbering, as he turned to face me now.

I looked into his face, handsome, full of authority and kindness, and, dear reader, I fainted!

As I came to, the man was leaning over me, cradling my head in his strong but gentle hands.

My throat felt dry as I gasped, 'Father?'

The man smiled benevolently down on me, and pulled my head to his breast. He just held me there, neither of us speaking.

As he loosened his grip, my wide open eyes surveyed him. 'Is this a trick? Are you a ghost?'

'Joshua, my Joshua, I am of flesh and blood in this realm. I am real. Oh my son, it is so good to see you and be able to hold you!'

'Father, what are you doing here?'

Lifting me to my feet, he chuckled, 'I might well ask you the same thing. I live here, Joshua – your mother and I – since...'

'Since you died.'

'Yes.'

I hesitated, my twelve-year-old brain struggling to take in this unexpected reunion with one I hardly knew, but loved deeply. 'You don't look dead.'

He let out a throaty, warm laugh. 'I am restored. I am dead to the world of men, but given new life here.'

'My grandfather wants to live forever.'

'So I gather.'

'But that is impossible, isn't it? He lost his immortality when he rebelled against the Pidaja.'

'There is a way that the life he seeks may not be lost to him.'

He looked now to the box on the table, and I followed his gaze to that small, beautiful casket.

My father spoke again. 'I know that you have come for this, Joshua, and you have been very brave and selfless to come this far.

'The Great I Am knows your grandfather's scheme and has done so since before it even formed in Primo Aquila's devious mind.'

'But, Father, that is what I do not understand. Why, when the Pidaja, the Great I Am, knows the evil plot to overthrow him, does he allow it to continue?'

Father curled one side of his mouth into a rueful smile. 'I rather think he wishes to teach your grandfather, my father, a lesson, Josh; a lesson in love.'

I did not understand, but perhaps I did not need to.

'Will the Great I Am kill me if I take the box to my grandfather?'

Father was silent for a moment. 'I really could not say. I would that you would stay here with me and be as one with I Am.'

'Can I see him?'

'Not now, but one day. He is extraordinary, cloaked in light and fire. It is he who is the light of this lighthouse and his flame is never extinguished. The daytime in the citadel never fades, and from here the light of he who is I Am shines into every dominion, penetrating the darkest places where lives are in danger of being dashed upon the rocks of pride, ignorance, fear. You cannot see him, and yet you can see by him everywhere. He illuminates all.'

I looked out from the lighthouse now. From the floors above, where I assumed the throne of I Am to be, a waterfall cascaded down the tower, plunging into a great river, as clear as crystal, flowing down the great street of the citadel. On each side of the river stood a great tree, bearing a dozen crops of fruit.

My father stood beside me as I wondered at this tree of life.

'Here, there is no pain, no curse. We need not the light of a lamp or the light of the sun, for he is light! Whatever your grandfather's schemes, I Am will reign forever! He is wonderful beyond your imagining. Stay with me, Joshua, with me and your mother.'

This place was like no other I had known, yet my heart was torn. 'But what about Lucy? She is alone and she needs me. I need her and if I return with the box, I may save our grandfather.'

My father looked dismayed. 'You may, although that rather depends on him. The choice is yours to make, my son.'

I looked at my feet, not being able to look him in the eye, and then I edged my way toward the centre of the room.

I laid my small, childish hand upon the exquisite oaken casket. It was cold to my touch, but my fingers caressed its intricate etchings and carvings. 'I must return, if there is even a glimmer of hope for my grandfather.'

Father sighed as I took the box from its resting place, 'Then your decision is made, dear son. I hope that your compassion may yet save the old fool. I cannot offer my protection over what may await you, Joshua, but you do go with my unceasing love.'

Tears welled in my eyes. 'Will I see you again, Father?'

He looked back across the city, avoiding my eye. 'I do not know.'

My heart broken at this last exchange, I turned to leave, before realising I was not quite sure how I could leave with no door or stairway.

My father was ahead of my thinking. 'Just take a step and you will be quite safe.'

'But Father, there is nothing but cloud; I will fall to the ground.'

'Oh, dear son, it is not cloud that wreathes this tower; those are angels, and they will bear you on their wings!'

SIXTY FOUR

LUCY SLAMMED THE DOOR behind her, her face reddened by tears, anger and the exertion of sprinting from the cliff top back to her room.

She hurried to the large four-poster bed at the centre of the room, and dropped to her knees, scrambling under the bed.

The floor was thick with dust, but she reached past the ancient, unused chamber pot, and wrestled out a large trunk, nearly as big as she was.

Lucy yanked the case up onto the bed, and plied open its rusting metal fastenings, flinging the lid open.

She went over to the dresser and took the few possessions she had, taking most special care over the set of clothes that Miss Tibbs had dressed her in on the day we were taken from our tranquil home and brought to Kerioth.

And then Lucy found my ill-fitting blazer that I had donned on that fateful day, and she sat on the bed and buried her head in the woollen garment, trying and failing to stifle her sobs.

After a few minutes she gathered herself and continued her packing, when there was a polite knock at the door.

She wilfully ignored it and closed the suitcase, awkwardly aligning the locks and clicking them into place.

The door behind her was pushed ajar, and Primo Aquila stood there, his twisted form dominating the room.

Lucy spoke first. 'There is nothing you can say to me. I am leaving here and you, and the only way you will stop me is by killing me, just as you killed Picardo and you killed Miss Tibbs, and my parents and everyone who has ever crossed you.'

Her rage was something to behold, but Aquila's response was measured, even muted, 'Lucy, I am dying. Please stay with me.'

'My brother is not coming back and I would rather go and live alone, anywhere, than spend another minute here with you.'

The daemon stumbled slightly forward – 'Lucy, please, I am dying!' – and then he fell forward onto his face.

'Your histrionics will not deter me, Mr. Aquila, for I will not call you my grandfather any further.' Then she turned to see him squirming on the floor, clutching for breath, his watch open in one hand, as the other clawed tormentedly at his chest.

The hands of the watch barely moved.

In a flash, Lucy rushed to his side, holding him in her arms, resting his head on her lap.

'Oh, Grandfather. Please don't die, not like this. Calm yourself, I will stay with you, I will stay.'

His charred black skin seemed pallid and clammy, cold beads of sweat collecting on his wrinkled, leathery face. The fire pits that were his eyes seemed to glow with just embers now.

'I have not got long, child. My days are swifter than a runner; they fly away without a glimpse of joy. They skim past like boats of papyrus, like eagles sweeping down on their prey. Unless your brother makes haste, the abyss is near for me.'

'What can I do for you, Grandfather, to make you better?'

'There is nothing that can be done, child.'

Lucy pondered a moment. 'When Joshua or I were ill, Miss Tibbs would sit up at night with us, dabbing a cloth to our brow, and praying for our recovery...' They looked directly at each other now. 'I would like to pray for you.'

The beleaguered old devil was silent for a moment, his every breath tortured, before he whispered, 'Very well.'

SIXTY FIVE

MY FEET HAD NO SOONER LEFT the wooden platform and stepped into the walls of cloud than I was immediately ensconced as though swaddled in a thick protective blanket.

The mortifying fear of stepping off a ledge into the unknown was instantly offset by the greatest sense of security and peace. I did not take time at that moment to consider that I was in the embrace of an angel, that the soft down I nestled my body into was the wings of an arch-prince of the Kaharian, holding me, guiding me safely down to terra firma. As soon as my feet touched the ground, the wisp of cloud released me and vanished into the 'walls' once more.

I was back in the square. Still the people danced, clapped, hugged and sang. Did they not realise that under my roughly hewn tunic I had secreted one of the deepest treasures of the Kaharian? The mystery of eternal life!

I made my way hurriedly across the square, trying not to meet anyone's eye or engage in their revelry.

Only once I was safely away from the crowds and back on the staircase did I take pause in a little alleyway to glance at my prize.

It was elegant and finely made, the oak making it seem heavier than its diminutive size suggested it might be, or maybe it was simply the burden of carrying it that made it seem weighty to me.

It was in many ways unremarkable. The kind of casket a well-to-do old lady of Miss Tibbs' acquaintance might keep loose-leaf tea in for occasions when she entertained guests.

If I had seen it on the shelves of the little collectors' shops that Tibbs frequented in search of her beloved thimbles, then I would not have given it a second glance.

Was this what my grandfather would have me risk all for?

I tried to prise open the polished silver clasp that fastened it shut. There was no lock, but it would not yield.

'I hope the secret inside is worth the effort!' I muttered to myself.

'What was that, young man?' I turned startled to see a smartly turned out elderly gentleman studying me through thick-lensed eye glasses.

I stowed the box back under my tunic.

'I am Ezekiel Boniface, young man,' he greeted me, offering his hand. 'I don't think I've had the pleasure of meeting you before, and I do like to make it my business to greet every soul who...'

But I did not hang around for him to complete his sentence. I hurtled down the marble steps, almost falling over my own feet on more than one occasion, bounding down the steps, one at a time, then two, then three. I had been discovered!

The old man Boniface shouted after me, though what he said I could not make out.

Passers-by turned to stare at the strangely dressed boy who scuttled down the stairs, fleeing from what, who could say? Even I was not sure but until that casket was in my grandfather's hands and I could feel the embrace of my sister once more, I would trust nobody, however good their intentions might be.

I bolted from the bottom step across the plaza. As I reached the spring of Gidron, I stumbled and fell. I landed flat in the water, face first, its icy coldness tantalising every muscle and sending it into chilly spasm. I splashed my way upright again, trying to catch my breath.

A number of onlookers had gathered by to witness this unaccustomed display of feverish indignity. I looked around and tried to force a smile of calm control and then I felt inside my tunic. The casket was gone!

I looked all around, dizzying myself by twisting and turning right and left, dunking my head back into the cold crystal flow of the spring.

All to no avail.

I wiped the water from my eyes, and found new wells started to flow as tears started to bubble.

I looked ahead, and saw there maybe ten feet away a gigantic, shoeless right foot.

I cast my gaze upwards to see the giant who towered above me. There, like a matchstick pinched between his massive fingers, it was held.

'Were you looking for this, young Master Joshua?' Araunah enquired.

'Please, Mr. Derwood, let me have the box and allow me through the gate. I do not expect you to understand, but I must get back, I need to get back home.'

The mighty giant bent down to me, offering me a finger to aid me from the stream. 'Oh, but I do understand. You forget I have a sibling too! Take your box, Master Joshua, and might it bring true life and love to those who would know its secrets!'

With immense strength he scooped me in one movement into his hand and over to the gate.

'Go in peace to love and serve the one who made you, young man.'

'How can I love him? I have not even met the one who made me!'

'Oh, but you have and you will! He is in all things. Why, you even bear the name the world will come to know him by!'

With that he picked me up by the scruff of the neck and lifted me over the gate tower, lowering me to safety on the other side.

Mr. Quibble had been dozing and woke with a start to see me airlifted into his field of vision.

He blustered as he unsteadily got to his feet. 'Do you have it?'

'I have it. Let us go.'

We started on our way back toward the garden at a brisk walk, Astrador in our tow, defending our rear, when it struck me that we were one member missing.

'Cara! Where is Cara?'

'She has gone on ahead of us to make safe the way. She had great confidence that you would come back with the casket.'

I was too on edge to beam with pride at this show of faith, but I beam now as I recall it.

'Talking of the casket, Master Joshua, may I see it? Or perhaps I could relieve you of the burden of carrying it for some little time?'

'No!' I snapped, unnecessarily harshly perhaps, 'It is quite safe with me, and we have not time to gawp and gaze upon it.'

Quibble did not respond, but looked away, pride possibly hurt.

Clouds started to gather above us, white at first, but then growing, darkening to slate grey.

Without a word, we hastened our pace. Rain was on its way; but what else?

HOURS, OR WHAT SEEMED LIKE HOURS, passed. The skies had opened upon us and we were wet through (although I was already soaked to the skin following my ungainly plummet into the spring).

We were now jogging, running away from the citadel, although no pursuit seemed to follow.

Pain tore into my sides, under the ribs; a stitch, but something more; a heaviness, not of limb, but of heart. I felt as though I was somehow older and older as I continued our journey.

And where was Cara? Surely we should have caught her by now, or she would have waited once the path was clear.

My mind was restless; I tried to keep focussed on the road ahead. We were on a different path to the one we approached the citadel on, and we circumvented Babel. I saw its tower and was reminded of the horrors that I had seen there.

My life, Cara, Lucy, our parents. Ageing, dying.

The nameless pain ripped through me again and I was thrown to the ground by its throes.

Quibble and Astrador immediately came to my aid, and as I looked up, I saw a look of terror across the face of the solicitor as he tended me.

'What is it?' I gasped through tremors of pain.

He averted his eyes. 'It is nothing, Master Joshua; it is only that you are much aged...'

I furrowed my brow at this odd statement, and lifted my hand up to the light. It was not my hand, not the hand I recognised, but the hand of an adult.

'This cannot be...'

'Master Joshua, will you not allow me to take the box for some while, to relieve you of this affliction, this enchantment.'

With what strength I had, I dragged myself to my feet. I did not answer his question. 'We must move forward, Mr. Quibble. En Gedi is in sight.'

I pressed on, my new, longer, full-grown legs carrying me faster, but the pain was growing in my belly, as though the earth was dragging me down by a chain.

On and on we went, my soul feeling heavier with every step, my legs feeling weaker, my skin tingling with a prickling heat.

We passed En Gedi by the morning light, and then we happened upon the threshold to Akeldama. The pain was too much and I dropped to the floor again, spread on my front, face to the dust.

Astrador nuzzled me in encouragement, rolling me onto my back. I looked up into his bright green eyes and stroked his face, and then I saw; my hand was gnarled and twisted, blue veins running like rivers along its length, the skin cracked and aged.

Astrador recoiled at the sight and I looked up into the skies. The rain ceased, but the clouds roared like a celestial bear and parted. There was an ear-piercing shriek. A scream so intense, so shattering, it was almost inaudible to my ears, but with a resonance that made the ground shake.

'Joshua! Quickly! The ground is breaking. I can see a portal ahead! We are almost home! Take my arm. We are almost home!'

I rolled onto my side, and saw a circular haze of blue on the horizon. Was that home? Could I dare to believe we were there?

My eyes were then taken by the land betwixt our position and our destination.

The cracked earth of Akeldama began to split and glow red from deep within its bowels.

Quibble helped my aged frame to the vertical, and draped my arm around his shoulder for support.

We started to make an unsteady path across the bloody field, the noxious gloop already lapping at our feet.

I screeched in pain as I felt as though something reached into my belly and started to pull from within, and then I saw there, from my stomach, a chain, golden in the eerie red light of the morning.

I felt as though some unseen force pulled me toward the ground. I struggled, with Quibble's help, to keep upright but the portal was still some distance ahead.

The blood began to flow and flow through the field and now there were just islands of land that we tried to hop between. Then there was another screech from above us – it was as though the skies were wailing a cacophonous war cry.

The earth beneath us shook, and from the rivers of blood they came, first hands, then heads, dragging themselves from the pit and thrusting their bloodied and charred bodies into the air.

There was an explosion of light above us, and a deafening clap of thunder as the pit creatures clashed with the clouds... not clouds, of course! Angels!

A battle raged above us as the hell hounds and the sentinels clashed in flashes of lighting, each thrust sending a shockwave blast of energy through the sky.

Creatures of all shapes and sizes continued to emerge from the rivers that were rapidly becoming a lake of blood.

Astrador now led the way, trying to find us a safe path, as Quibble helped me struggle on.

We were getting close to the portal. Close to home.

I went to take another step toward safety, when I found my feet would not move.

I looked down to see a bloodied arm wrapped around my chain like a tentacle, clinging, grasping to regain its life... or to take mine. The slimy, slithering hand wound itself around the chain like a barbed snake, clawing at the links, gripping.

At once, Astrador was at hand, teeth bared, claws unleashed; he ripped into the arm, causing it to flinch, squirm and slither back from whence it came.

I slumped to the ground, the energy gone from my body.

'Master Joshua, please, take my arm, we are so close!' the good solicitor implored.

'I cannot! I am too weak, too tired.'

'Then let me take the box, relieve you of this heavy burden, and let us get to safety.'

I looked into his eyes and sensed something I had not for some time.

'I do not trust you. I do not trust my grandfather. You shall not have it!'

'Joshua, please! I am your friend. You will have us all die if you do not let me carry it.'

'Then I choose a mortal death! I will not choose what is easy, I choose what is right...'

'What madness is this!'

'I will stay and learn of the Great I Am! I will abide in him! He is light and he is life! I am going back to the citadel and the box is coming with me!'

I gathered all the strength I could find in my haggard old legs and lifted myself up. My resolve seemed to energise me. I was not afraid.

Quibble grabbed my shoulder. As I turned to meet his gaze, his eyes were black like flint.

'Joshua, my Master will not be thwarted...'

There was no pain, and his movement was too swift or my reflexes too dulled to see the blade, but it slid between my ribs with cold, ruthless efficiency.

For a moment I stayed standing, almost unbelieving, and Quibble grabbed me by my tunic as he slid his hand into the opening and took what he sought.

Neither of us spoke, our eyes locked on one another, Astrador was quite unaware, I am sure, that anything untoward had occurred. Then Quibble loosened his grip and I slid backwards to the ground and toward the deepening blood at our feet.

I looked up to see the toad-man I had taken for a friend disappear through the misty blue oval of light as I looked down to see drips of my own blood trickling, merging into the sea that surrounded me.

I felt warm, I felt safe, as I lay back, my eyes looking up to the sky. There were sparks of lightning throughout the sky as the battle raged around, soundless to my ears.

The lights of the battle began to dim as a haze of red covered me and I felt my eyes become heavy and close.

My world became silent, even the sound of my own breath disappeared. All was black.

All, except for one small imprint on my vision, barely a trace, but there, fleetingly, the outline of a winged deer swooping down.

And then it was gone.

Sixty Six

THE FIRE WAS COUGHING and spluttering on its last few logs. It was enough to illuminate the otherwise darkened room, and the two figures who sought only warmth and comfort from its meagre flame.

Primo Aquila was lying prostrate on a chaise close to the fire's glow and at his side my sister sat upright, tending him, dabbing his sweating brow and urging him to sip from a glass of water. He dribbled as he took each slurp, too weak to lift his head.

His breath was tortured and wheezing, the pause between each seemingly becoming longer, causing Lucy to tense as she feared it might be the last that he breathed.

Not a word passed between them. What was there to say? It had been months since Quibble and I had passed through fire and water into the mysterious land that lay beyond. What hope was there?

The silence hung heavily in the room, it reeked of utter despair.

The fire gave a little cough as though it might flicker and die, but then another cough, followed by a torrent of flame and at its centre spewed forth the familiar rotund shape of Innocent Quibble.

Lucy started at this horrible apparition. Quibble was robed, covered in blood, soot and sweat. He stood in the hearth panting and clutching something in his right hand.

Primo Aquila looked up, his eyes widened and like a flash he was on his feet, enlivened by a renewed vigour; a new hope.

'Oh, my dear friend. That which you carry...' – he licked his lips, alive with anticipation – 'is it that of which we have spoken;

the time capsule in which the greatest secret I would have in my possession may become known to me?'

'Where is Joshua?' Lucy interjected, but her question went unheard among the silent but giddy delirium that passed between the two men.

'Sire, it is!' Quibble fell to one knee offering the oak casket to his master.

Aquila immediately reached out to grab it, then at the last moment slowing his move, wishing to savour the sensation.

His spindly fingers grasped the square end of the wooden box, and he drew in a deep, long breath, before casting his face upwards and letting out a hellish, whooping holler.

'Oh for so long I have been the slave of time, and now I shall become its master!

'All shall bow before me' – he pointed to some imagined point above him in the sky – 'and you, oh Pidaja, who turned his most beautiful creations into the dogs of the pit, you will know my justice when the wheel has turned. You will grovel in the dirt, chained by seconds and minutes and hours, while I will become infinite and eternal! Behold!'

He clasped the box tightly to his chest with both hands, planting kisses on its unspoiled surface with his thin, ugly lips. With reverence, he placed the casket on a small table, and retreated from it a step or two, before extending his arm before him and pointing a long, spindly digit at its lock.

'Shemaniathak!' he roared, and a flash of lightning flew forth from his finger toward the box.

There was a spark of flame and the lid of the casket flew open amid a small cloud of dust and smoke.

Lucy and Quibble stood like statues in terrified silence as the old daemon started to emit a small chuckle which rose and rose to a crescendo of cacophonous howling, chilling in its malevolence.

He managed to control his grimly victorious mirth and gave a little clap of his hands like a child opening his favourite sweets.

He turned now to my petrified sister. 'My dear, I would like you to have the honour of passing the contents of the box to me.'

'Where is my brother?'

'Very well, if you will dwell on such trivialities at a time such as this, I will do it myself.

'My thanks to you, Mr. Quibble, you have been faithful to the last, and you will be rewarded for your loyalty.'

'You are gracious indeed, my Lord.'

Primo Aquila stepped toward the box, his eyes burning with lust. His lust was dampened somewhat as he removed the contents, however.

'What is this, I wonder?'

He took a small package from the casket, which was wrapped in purple satin. He laid it on the table and folded back the edges of the wrapping.

A book, with something written on the cover.

'No, this cannot be! This is a trick – I cast this onto the fire!' He stammered for breath as Quibble moved to the table to see what had caused his master such distress.

Quibble read aloud from the cover: '"Whoever believes in him shall not perish, but have eternal life!"' He did a double take, and then began to leaf through the pages of the thick leather-bound volume.

'It cannot be!' repeated Aquila, reeling at the simplicity of the box's contents.

'What is it?' said Lucy, her reverie broken by the drama that was unfolding.

'Why, Miss Lucy,' said the solicitor, 'it is your father's copy of the scripture. The secret must be hidden within it!'

My grandfather sat now on the chaise, motionless, 'No, you fat fool. You do not have to search for the secret. The scripture is the secret! Read what it says: "Whoever believes in him shall not perish..."'

'"...but have eternal life!"' Quibble continued. 'Oh my Lord, then it is accomplished! You need only repent, ask forgiveness of the Great I Am, and he will restore you to life. He is extending the gift of love even to you...'

Aquila leapt to his feet. 'Silence! How dare you speak to me of repentance and forgiveness and love! Even if I washed myself with soap and my hands with cleansing powder, he would plunge me into a slime pit so that even my clothes would detest me. He is not a mere mortal that I might answer him, that we might confront each other in court! I loved he who is I Am once and he sought the pitiful selfish love of you ignorant humans. I will never bow to him again. Look at what he has made me, and now he will kill me…'

'Repent, Grandfather!' Lucy begged him.

'No more!' he defended, curling his fists into tight balls.

'Repent, Master, and live anew!' Quibble jabbered.

'Never!' Aquila lashed out knocking the solicitor to the floor. 'I will not live to have the life of the slave! I will be the Master! I will not kneel to anyone!' He raised his hand again to strike a death blow to Quibble's temple, when he suddenly staggered backwards with a hideous scream: 'Aaaaggghhhh!'

He clutched his chest with clawing fingers, a horrible retching in his throat. He pulled the watch from his pocket and looked at it, his face frozen. It had stopped.

His knees buckled beneath him and his tall, gangling frame struck the floor with a deathly thud.

Lucy, dear sweet Lucy, rushed to his side, and stroked his face. He looked upon her once more and tried to smile, but the pain was too great.

'Grandfather, you have gained the secret. Put aside your pride, please repent.'

'You are a good person, Lucy. I, alas, am not.'

'I love you. I can't bear to think you will just cease to be. Please, please, repent and live, if not in this world, then the next.'

'Ah, dear Lucy, I…'

But the words never came.

Epilogue

I DO NOT KNOW HOW LONG passed from when the winged deer left my vision. In death, time loses its rigidity somewhat.

All I know is that there was a time of darkness. I was still aware of being, but devoid of feeling. When my eyes opened I was still looking to the sky, the battle-scarred clouds now dispersed and uninterrupted blue in their stead.

I had no feeling in my body but I felt no distress, no compulsion to move from the balmy embrace of tranquil slumber.

Into the corner of my vision there came a shadow. No, not a shadow; a presence of light, and a presence that was familiar to me.

She did not speak, but as her hand soothed my brow, I knew I was safe.

'It is good to see you, Miss Tibbs... or do I call you Tibethia?'

The old lady moved into my eyeline, although no longer old: young, beautiful and ethereal.

'It is good to see you as well, Joshua.'

'Where am I?'

'You are at the citadel.'

'I fell into the river, the blood.'

'And you were lifted from it...'

'Cara! Then I am alive?' I questioned hopefully.

'More than ever, and yet not as you would understand it. When the storm has swept by, the wicked are gone, but the righteous stand firm forever. You did a very noble thing, Joshua, you stood in the way of lust for power and deceit, and chose to follow a selfless course, whatever the cost to yourself.'

I lifted my head and began to get my bearings. Tibbs offered me her fair hand and I took it – she was deceptively strong!

As I rose, I felt a searing pain between my shoulder blades, and I winced.

'Ah, you will get used to that, dear, as all our kind must.'

'Our kind?' I questioned, but received no reply. I felt a load on my back and reached around... feathers! I had feathers, and if I had feathers then I must have...

'Now, Joshua, there are some people who would like to see you.'

I followed Tibbs' eyeline and saw some little way in the distance the unmistakable figure of the Doe of the Morning, and my heart leapt for joy! Beside her was a man, simply dressed and seemingly unremarkable. I had never seen him before and yet I knew him. I could only smile at his presence, and then I began to sing.

SO HERE ENDS THE CHRONICLE of the journey I took. This ending is not *the* end of course, as I write this account many years on, and many more events have passed for better and for worse.

I never did have the chance to be with my sister again, to share her company, to make her laugh, or to wind her up until her face rouged with irritation at my childish pranks. I still see her but she does not, cannot, see me. She is still beautiful.

She never married but surrounded herself with books of scripture, thimbles, and a miniature domesticated pantera named Astrador (yes, he made it back!) and she prays each day for the souls of those she has lost. She prays for those who are in need, and often her prayers are answered, even if she does not know it. She is lonely, but she is never alone.

Mr. Quibble never did tell Lucy the secret of how I met my fate. Perhaps it is best she never knew. In any case, his remorse in later years was heartfelt and he made his peace with his creator long ago. He again taught others the stories of the Kaharian and became a wonderful husband, and a devoted, loving father to that strange ape-boy. He thought the world of him, and took him on long walks in the parks, never stopping to hear the sniping insults of passers-by. He saw only beauty in his son.

As for me, well, I take my post on the walls of the citadel and I keep watch over those I am entrusted to protect. It gives me joy to serve and to keep safe those who ask for the protection of the Kaharian. Every now and then, normally as the day breaks, from my station on the battlements I see the happy sight of the Doe of the Morning grazing in the garden and I go to her, and we talk, and we sing. Those moments of companionship take my breath away.

I seek no more. I could have no more than to walk in the ways of the Great I Am.

My grandfather was a daemon. I am an angel.

AND WHAT OF THAT DAEMON, the angel who fell from his lofty height as a result of his overwhelming pride?

I simply do not know.

I look out over the world, but do not see into the citadel, which is under the sole protection of I Am. Who walks its streets is beyond my sight.

Whether his incomplete final sentence in life ever reached a repentant conclusion in death I do not know. I can only hope.

In either case, even if his everlasting life was not won by my sister's unceasing loving kindness, I do believe both were changed for the better by the love that passed between them.

The secret of eternal life is available to all who seek it. There is no longer a gateway at Kerioth between the world of men and the Kaharian, but as Araunah Derwood prophesied to me at the Gidron spring, one did come into the world of men, bearing my name. He broke the chains of mortality and he became the doorway to a full and everlasting life, through the simple act of believing.

There is a door in the world. Knock, and the door will be opened!